Dragon Blood Chronicles 2:
Betrayed

Dragon Blood Chronicles 2: Betrayed

Avril Sabine

Cracked Acorn Productions
Australia

Dragon Blood Chronicles 2: Betrayed

Published by

Cracked Acorn Productions

PO Box 1365

Gympie, Queensland 4570

Australia

978-1-925617-79-5 (Kindle)

978-1-925617-80-1 (EPUB)

978-1-925617-81-8 (Print)

Genre: Young Adult Urban Fantasy

Copyright 2018 © Avril Sabine

Cover design by Caitlyn Petersen

All rights reserved

*For Mum, who is thankfully nothing like
Brigitte.*

When one of the few people Morgane trusts is taken from her, all she should be able to think of is revenge. Not the pain of losing them. As a Gold Dragon, she can't show weakness. That will get her killed. Is she more human, than dragon, like her mother has always accused? When it comes to survival of the fittest, being compared to a human can make other dragons see you as an easy target. And that isn't something she's going to let happen. The only problem is, she has no idea how to prevent it.

*

This story was written by an Australian author using Australian spelling.

Name Pronunciation

Like many names there is more than one way to pronounce the following ones. These are the pronunciations used in this story.

Names:

Anja (ann-jah)

Ari (rhymes with harry)

Becan (beck-ann)

Brigitte (brish-eet)

Cort (rhymes with caught)

Devona (de-vone-ah)

Elin (e-lin)

Jorn (rhymes with thorn)

Gwynham (gwin-hem)

Hella (hel-la)

Mikkel (mick-ell)

Morgane (more-gain)

Starne (star-n)

Tarben (tar-bin)

Tathen (tath-en)

Other pronunciations:

Pliethin (plea-thin)

Chapter One

Morgane followed Anja through the forest, her longbow in her left hand, her quiver and sheathed dagger at her right hip. Anja's slim figure slipped past bushes and trees, her body avoiding touching them and leaving signs of her passage behind. She carried the same weapons as Morgane and her shirt, trousers and supple leather boots were the browns of the forest, her dark brown hair blending in equally as well.

Morgane, who wore the same coloured clothes, looked over her shoulder to check that Elin followed. Elin was similar in appearance and build to Anja. Although rather than the blue of Anja's eyes, Elin's were brown, similar to Morgane's. Except Elin didn't have the flecks of gold that were scattered throughout the brown of her eyes. Elin and Anja were cousins, but similar enough in appearance they could have been sisters.

Elin grinned. "Better watch where you're going."

Facing forward, Morgane tried to avoid a branch. It caught on the brown, leather scarf wrapped around her head. Her white blond hair cascaded around her shoulders and down her back, dragged out of a twisted coil by the same branch.

At Elin's laughter, Anja stopped and faced them. She grinned. "Better hide your hair before you become the prey."

Elin slung her longbow over her shoulder and took the scarf off the branch. "Let me help you. We're too close to the village for you to leave your hair uncovered." She wrapped Morgane's hair around her head in a tight coil before fixing the scarf over it. Smiling, she tucked a loose strand beneath the thin, soft leather. "There you go. Not even one of our hunters would be able to spot you now."

Morgane couldn't help glancing in the direction of the village her friends came from. She saw only trees and bushes. Not a single hunter. She gestured in the opposite direction. "We should probably separate here anyway. I need to head home."

Anja slung her longbow over her shoulder and threw her arms around Morgane. "Next time, we should go for a month instead of only a week. A week isn't long enough." Her arms tightened around Morgane. "You should have been a hunter. You'd have made a better hunter than a dragon."

Morgane returned the hug, dreading the thought of facing her mother after being gone for a week. She also ignored the comment about being a hunter. She was a dragon. There were things about being a hunter she would have liked, but she'd never want to give up being a dragon to become one. And she'd told her friends that numerous times. Letting go of Anja, she stepped back. "I might not be able to see you for a couple of weeks." She hadn't told either of them that she'd left without permission. Nor was she about to. "It's the day of our birth tomorrow. Mine and Gwynham's." She grinned at the thought of her twin brother and the effort he'd gone to in helping her sneak out of the castle. He didn't think she should spend time with hunters, but that didn't stop him from helping her. "I'm sure there are things I'll need to catch up on after being away for so long."

Anja looked over Morgane's shoulder, in the direction of the castle. "What are they like? Celebrations at the castle. Do the rest of the dragons kill young villagers and drink their blood from gold goblets?"

Morgane laughed. "Of course they don't. Are you sure you didn't make that up? Or the rest of the rumours you tell me about."

Anja shared a look with Elin who shrugged.

Morgane looked from one to the other. "What is it?"

Elin shook her head, hugging her tightly before stepping back. "Nothing. Enjoy your celebrations tomorrow. If you were from our village, there'd be no celebrations. Not until you returned from the sacred waters in the mountains."

"Even then there might not be any celebrations," Anja said flatly.

Elin draped an arm around Anja's shoulders. "I'm sorry. I shouldn't have mentioned-"

Anja interrupted Elin. "I have to get over it some time. I'm confronted with magic nearly every moment of the day."

"Except this past week," Elin said softly.

Morgane wished she could say something to cheer Anja. But there was nothing she could say. How did you comfort someone who faced a life without magic when it was such an integral part of their society?

A sound had the three of them facing the direction of the village. Relief at seeing a deer caused them to laugh softly. The laughter faded when an arrow struck the deer, dropping it to the ground.

Anja took a step towards Morgane, turning her to face the direction of the castle. "Go. If they see you…" She let her warning trail off.

With one last glance over her shoulder, Morgane ran in the direction of the castle, snatching her scarf from a branch as it was again tugged from her hair. She shoved it in her belt pouch, not slowing her pace. The trees pressed in too close for her to shapeshift. Not that she'd consider changing into her dragon form to fly the rest of the way to the castle. The less attention she drew to herself returning home, the better. If she was lucky, she'd manage to sneak inside and find her brother so she could learn when their mother had discovered she was missing. And make sure their stories matched. Who knew what he'd come up with in his efforts to keep their mother from learning when she'd left and where she'd gone.

She doubted Gwynham would have been able to hide the fact for more than a day or two. A soft sound had her dodging to the side and she glanced at an arrow that embedded itself in a tree in front of her. Straining her ears, she tried to hear who followed. The myriad sounds of the forest were loud when she focused. Creatures scurrying about, larger creatures fleeing the area and birds taking flight. Yet she couldn't hear the one who hunted her. She breathed in deep, trying to catch their scent. A mixture of smells assaulted her.

Nearby was death, overpowering the sweet smells released by the plants her feet crushed as she ran across them. Another soft sound had her dodging in the other direction. The sound of an arrow impaling a tree had her glancing over her shoulder. There was nothing. No movement, no visible hunter. Not that she'd expected to see them. With their magic to keep them silent and their ability to slip unnoticed through the forest, hunters could hide in plain sight. Even those not using magic to hide themselves were nearly impossible to find.

She slipped around a broad tree, hearing an arrow embed itself in the wood on the other side of the trunk. Sinking low to the ground, she moved slowly towards a shrub. She forced her breathing to slow and strained her ears for the slightest of sounds. Crouching behind the shrub, she heard it. Not the hunter. No, the creatures scurrying out of the way.

Placing her bow on the ground beside her, she wrapped her hair around her head, hiding the bright strands beneath the scarf she took from her belt pouch. She felt along the edges, making sure every strand was hidden. Again she tried to hear where the hunter might be. Nothing. Not the whisper of sound, not something cracking beneath a footstep or even the whistle of an arrow through the air. There was silence. An unnatural silence as not even the small creatures remained nearby.

Holding her breath, she peered around the edge of the shrub. Scanning the area, she looked for depressions in the ground where a hidden hunter might be standing. She'd practised tracking Elin. Her friend wasn't officially a hunter. Hadn't yet turned eighteen and visited the sacred waters in the mountains. But she would gain that status when she made the journey. And as she practised and her magic improved, she'd be able to bend the light around her for greater periods of time to remain hidden for longer than what she was currently capable of.

A hunter appeared in front of Morgane, his bow drawn back, an arrow aimed at her. She recognised him instantly. Elin's brother. Jorn. She froze, staring into the dark brown eyes, so similar to his sister's. His hair, a slightly darker shade to Elin's, fell in tousled waves around his face. He wore similar clothes to hers, forest browns, and had a quiver of arrows and a sheathed dagger at his right hip, belt pouch on his left and supple leather boots on his feet. He had the typical, close cropped beard that circled his mouth and chin and went along his jawline, as many of the males in the village wore.

She tensed, ready for him to let go of the string. Yet he continued to stand in front of her. What was he waiting for? Then she realised. For his magic to allow him to go invisible again. Wrapping a hand around her bow, that rested on the ground, she launched herself towards him, grabbing the arrow from the air as he let go of the string. Dropping the arrow, she threw herself at him, changing enough to allow claws to puncture his flesh. The sharp scent of blood filled her senses. Releasing him, she raced through the forest, bringing her fingers to her lips, licking the blood from them, savouring and learning all she could of him. Taste, scent, form, mind, location. Not as efficient as the mage trackers Gilda had told her about, but more than sufficient for what she needed.

There was no way he'd be able to hide from her now. She could feel the tug of him behind her, the sense of him. She veered away. He followed. The distance between them decreased. Slipping her bow across her head and shoulder, she positioned it on her back and leapt for the branch of a nearby tree, scurrying up it. She sensed him slow. He'd lost her.

A smile slowly formed as she sensed him below. Invisible.

He walked around the tree, slight depressions in the ground giving him away now she knew where he was. There was only silence from his location. Complete and utter silence. A sound in the distance caught her attention. A sound in the direction of the castle. He was too close to where her mother's warriors patrolled. And he was only a hunter, didn't have her sense of smell and hearing. One hunter didn't stand a chance against five dragon warriors. Even warriors that weren't Gold. Maybe an older hunter's magic would be powerful enough to take on five dragons, but not the magic of a twenty-year-old.

Jorn appeared below her, scanning the area as he moved slowly around the tree, frowning. She couldn't resist a smile. It faded as quickly as it had appeared. If it wasn't for the warriors headed towards them, she could have outwaited him. If she stayed in the tree Jorn was as good as dead. There was no way she could face Elin if she sat by and watched Elin's brother killed.

If she called down and warned him, the warriors would hear. There was even a chance they'd hear if she dropped down in front of him and whispered a warning in his ear. They were close. Too close.

Jorn turned in the direction of the warriors. He took a step towards them.

Had he heard something? She didn't know and couldn't risk him heading that way thinking it was her. There was only one thing she could do. And it should work. Weren't the villagers human, like the servants her grandfather had left here with her mother? Forming claws, she pierced the skin of her wrist before leaping softly to the ground below. Straightening, she knocked the arrow from Jorn's hand when he spun to face her, pressing the blood on her fingers against his lips.

Staggering back, he wiped a hand across his mouth.

She grinned. His action was too late. Some of her blood had already entered his mouth. Spinning, she raced through the forest sensing him follow. Behind him, she heard the warriors veer in their direction. *"Jorn."* She sent her thoughts into his mind, the link opened by his consumption of her blood.

"Get out of my head. Dragon."

"Five warriors chase you."

"Impossible. They can't hear me. Or see me."

"But they can hear me." He didn't answer her and it was only that she could sense he followed that she knew he was behind her. *"Jorn. Go home."*

"I'll go home if you stay away from my sister."

Laughter nearly escaped. *"This is for her sake I warn you. Do you think she'd want you killed?"*

"She says you're her friend. Not much of a friend if you're willing to let her be ostracised from the village and unable to make the journey to the sacred waters."

His words caused her to stumble. *"What do you mean?"*

There was a moment of silence before Jorn replied. *"I should have known she wouldn't have told you."*

She entered a clearing, large enough she'd be able to shapeshift. She didn't slow her pace. *"Then how about you tell me."* She sensed him enter the clearing. Well over halfway across it, she stopped and turned to face him. Once more he was invisible. She heard the arrow whistle through the air before she saw it, sidestepping before it could strike her. *"Show yourself."* She latched the top of her specially designed quiver into place. *"If you don't, I could hurt you."* Her clothes and weapons might look like those of the villagers, but they were different. Made from dragon-leather. As was her scarf, which had been made from the thinnest of leather.

Jorn appeared, his bow drawn back an arrow pointed at her again. *"Not before I can hurt you."* He let go of the string and the arrow flew towards her.

Chapter Two

Morgane jumped into the air, shapeshifting into a silver dragon with golden wing veins and flecks of gold across her scales. She scooped Jorn off the ground, her claws wrapping around his arms. Her grip was awkward, but she couldn't improve the position while she flew across the treetops. She banked to the right, flying towards the mountains she could see in the distance. She could feel a slight sting along her arm and guessed the arrow had grazed her.

"You'll pay for this," Jorn warned.

"You have no idea." If the warriors had spotted her, they'd carry the tale to her mother. She'd been forbidden to associate with the villagers. All the villagers. Including her two friends. It wasn't acceptable behaviour for a dragon. Especially a Gold Dragon.

"*Set me down. Now.*" Jorn stayed still, gripping his bow.

Scanning the forest below, she could see nowhere large enough to land. Spying a river, glinting in the sun, she flew in that direction. Maybe the banks would be clear enough for her to land.

"*Are you listening to me, Dragon?*"

"*It's Morgane.*"

"*Do you think I care what your name is? Set me down. Now.*"

"*The only way you're going to get on the ground is if I drop you. There's nowhere large enough for me to land. I don't know this area well enough to find somewhere suitable.*" She should have gone in the direction she'd travelled during the past week. There'd been a few clearings her and the hunters had camped in. She felt Jorn twist in her grip. "*Don't move if you don't want to be dropped.*"

"*When the river forks into two, follow the right hand one. A little way along it the forest thins, becoming rockier. Head further to the right and you'll see a plateau with very little vegetation on it. You can land there.*"

She'd already started along the right hand fork of the river before he'd finished his directions. "*Are you crazy? Savages live out that way.*"

"Savages are preferable to putting up with your company."

She tried not to let his words hurt. They stung worse than the arrow she'd been shot with. Reaching the plateau, she scanned the ground before she landed, letting go of him first. Becoming human again, she checked the wound on her arm. Like she'd guessed, it was a graze, having done more damage to her shirt than her skin. Seeing him take another arrow from his quiver, she sighed. There was no one in the area, so she was able to speak aloud. "That is getting very annoying." She nodded towards his bow.

"Stay out of my sister's life and I won't have to kill you." He drew back the arrow.

"Do you think your sister would be happy if you killed me?" she demanded.

"I'm sure she'll get over it." He let go of the string, reaching for another arrow.

Ready for it, she grabbed the arrow from the air and threw herself at him, wrapping her arms around him, having knocked the second arrow from his hand, she held on tightly. "Have you forgotten I'm stronger than you?"

"Have you forgotten I can use magic?"

She grinned up at him. She knew a lot more about his capabilities then he did about hers. Elin and Anja had shared many of their secrets with her. And she'd shared some of her own in return. "Not without hurting yourself."

"What has Elin told you?"

She felt his muscles tense against her body. Yet he didn't try to escape. Was he planning something? Did he truly know she was stronger than him? "No more than I told them."

"Did you tell them how to kill you?"

She kept her expression blank. A trick she'd had plenty of experience with over the years. Even though they were a long way from their own lands, and had no way to return to them, her mother firmly believed in survival of the fittest. And that meant showing no weakness. Especially around other dragons. "Why don't you ask Elin?" She would have preferred to ask what was the best way to kill him. She kept the question to herself. Maybe he'd let something slip if he thought she knew more than she did. Not that she'd be able to kill him. Elin and Anja would be devastated if she did.

"Let me go. I'll give you my word not to attack you long enough for you to leave if you promise not to return," Jorn said.

Looking deep into his eyes, she saw only anger. She was tempted to sift through his mind to see if she could get past the surface thoughts to the private ones beneath. A sound caught her attention and she breathed in deeply, the scents of the area assaulting her senses. "I can't do that."

"Why not?"

"Because the plateau isn't as empty as it initially was." She should have been paying better attention. A dozen savages shouldn't have had the chance to creep so close. She mentally ran through the possibilities. There was no way both of them could escape unharmed. Only her and she wasn't about to leave Jorn to face the savages since she was the one who'd carried him away from the forests around his village.

He tried to pull away from her. "Let me go." He reached for an arrow.

"Go invisible." Letting him go, she spun to face the direction of the savages, shapeshifting as she did. Launching into the air, she batted away the spears that were thrown at her. A glance below showed Jorn was invisible and she sensed he'd moved to the side.

Morgane dived towards one of the savages, aiming for the next savage when an arrow impaled the first one. She landed on the second savage, her claws tearing at his skin before she flew into the sky, dodging more spears. So much for being home before the middle of the day like she'd told her brother. She'd be lucky to arrive before the sun set.

Again she dived towards the savages. Once more it was one Jorn attacked. She angled away, barely avoiding being struck by spears. *"How about you attack the ones on the right and I'll go for the ones on the left?"*

"How about we swap that?"

Roaring, she aimed for the savages on the right, claws sinking into the chest of one of them before she angled skywards again. *"Was there a reason my plan wasn't good enough for you?"*

"Yeah, if I go for the ones aiming for you, they won't see my arrows coming."

Banking, she flew towards the savages, pulling up at the last moment when she saw more in the distance. *"We have to go. There's about thirty of them headed this way."*

"Why don't you leave?"

"Elin is my friend."

"What about Anja?"

She hadn't been certain he'd known about Anja. *"Both of them. I'd never do anything that would hurt either of them."* She flew towards where she sensed him. *"Including letting someone they care about die. Can you swim?"*

"Yes."

"Hold your hands above your head. Make sure they're empty and become visible when I tell you 'now'."

"Why?"

She dodged a spear that was thrown at her, flying towards him. *"Now."* She was surprised he obeyed. Grabbing hold of his hands, she flew higher, heading for the river before she dived towards the ground, letting go of him to become human. They both landed in the water. Surfacing, she looked in his direction.

The water was up to his chest and he glared at her. "I hope you don't expect my thanks."

She grinned, brushing strands of hair away from her face and capturing the scarf before it floated away. She slipped it inside her belt pouch. "Not at all." She stared at him for a moment. There was no way she could leave him out in the middle of nowhere. If something happened, neither Elin nor Anja would forgive her. She doubted she'd forgive herself either. Not for getting Jorn killed. She didn't know him well enough to care if he lived or died. No, for the pain it'd cause her friends.

Jorn reached for the bow slung across his back.

She moved quicker than him, wrapping a hand around his wrist and preventing him from getting his weapon.

"I'll take you with me." Fire pooled in his hand.

She met his gaze, seeing the determination in his dark eyes. "The only place I plan to take you is closer to your village."

"Why?" The flames remained in his hand.

She focused on his face, refusing to show fear at the magic he continued to hold. She'd seen what their magic could do to dragons. Not personally. In images shared by dragons that had been with her mother from the beginning. Been here when the world had closed in upon itself, preventing any of the dragons from leaving or more coming. "I've already told you. For Elin. And Anja."

The flames dwindled to nothing. "Then why did we need to land?" He glanced down. "In freezing cold water."

She pressed a hand against his chest, moving close when he tried to step away. "I didn't realise you were cold. Are you too cold for me to take you into the sky?"

"The sooner we can part company, the better."

Again she ignored the sting his words caused. It was this kind of attitude that made it impossible for her to visit Elin and Anja's village. Inclining her head, she let go of his hand and stepped away. "When I shapeshift, the string of my bow will be like it's part of me, but the bow itself will remain between my wings for you to hold onto. Do not damage my wings when you climb on or it will be I who takes you with me."

"I'm ready to leave."

She checked him over one more time, hoping he wouldn't do anything stupid like shred her wings and cause both of them to die. Changing forms, she held her wing out of the way to allow him to clamber onto her back. *"Are you holding on?"*

"Yes."

She launched into the air, shooting skywards. Not wanting to risk catching anyone's attention, she flew higher, the trees dwindling away below her. It took a moment to realise Jorn was shivering. She could hear his teeth chattering. Scanning the area below, she recognised one of the clearings well off towards the mountains. Changing directions, she headed towards it. There was a cave she'd stayed in during the week she'd been away.

"Where are you going?"

She barely understood the words through the chattering of his teeth. *"We'll stop long enough for you to get warm and then I'll take you closer to your village."*

This time, he spoke in her mind. *"There's no need. I can last long enough to get home."*

"I won't be able to take you into your village. You'll still have a fair walk. There's a cave at the edge of the clearing up ahead." She flew lower, heading towards it.

"I know the one you mean. We use it when we're hunting around here. We don't need to stop. You can take me home. I can manage to walk from wherever you leave me."

She didn't bother answering, landing at the edge of the clearing closest to the cave. Anja had been chilled as bad as this when she was younger and had been sick for weeks, the healers struggling to cure her. Did he want the same to happen to him?

"Did you hear me?"

"Unless you want to be on my back when I shapeshift, I suggest you get off." She began to think he wasn't going to move and was about to tell him again.

He nearly fell off her back, catching himself at the last moment to land on his feet. The chattering of his teeth had lessened, but it was more noise than he normally made. "We don't need to stop."

She shapeshifted so she could speak aloud. "I'll gather firewood."

He grabbed hold of her shoulder turning her to face him. "Stop ignoring me."

She twisted her shoulder out of his grip. "Then stop making stupid comments." She turned away, gathering various sized sticks. She glanced at him when he joined her. "Can you light a fire with your magic?"

"That's not necessary. I always carry a flint and steel with me." His hand brushed the belt pouch at his left hip before bending to pick up a small branch.

They gathered wood in silence, taking it back to the cave where Morgane laid the fire in the opening.

"Do you ever listen to anyone?" His teeth no longer chattered, but he shivered regularly.

She looked up at him with a grin. "Only if they're right."

"How would you recognise that? It would involve admitting you might be wrong."

Chapter Three

Morgane stared at Jorn for a moment trying to figure out if that had been a touch of humour she'd glimpsed in his eyes. It had to have been with how dry his tone had been. She rose to her feet, gesturing towards the wood she'd laid for the fire. "Want to light it?"

He took out a flint and steel and crouched by the wood. "Why not turn into a dragon and set it on fire?"

She didn't have that ability. There were no Pliethins in this world. It was one of her mother's biggest complaints, right after the fact that her father had dumped her here and the dragon who'd promised to find a way to help her escape had never turned up. Her and Gwynham's father. The dragon her mother refused to speak about other than for threats of what she'd do to him if she ever saw him again. The only dragon in this world who could breathe fire was

Dorran. The rest of the Golds had been killed by hunters from the local village when they'd first arrived.

Jorn looked up from the fire he'd lit. "No comment?"

Hearing his stomach grumble, she gestured towards the fire. "You keep that burning and I'll bring something to cook on it." Leaving the cave, she shapeshifted, focusing on sound and smell, searching out the closest prey. She flew across the clearing, keeping low to the ground and landing as she reached the treeline. She shapeshifted to slip between the trees and grab a rabbit that tried to escape. Grinning, she sauntered back to the campfire that was now burning brightly. Her grin faded when another smell came to her. The scent of blood. No sounds accompanied it. That could mean only one thing. Tossing the rabbit by the fire, she left the cave again. "You clean it. I'll be back soon." She leapt into the air, shapeshifting before he could speak.

"Where are you going?" He was forced to speak with his mind since she was already far into the sky.

"There's another hunter in the area."

"How do you know?"

"I could smell the blood of their kill." She circled far above the land, searching for the hunter. She didn't

see them until they were nearly at the fire. A young man probably a couple of years older than Jorn. He carried a deer slung across his shoulders. *"Do you know him? Are you safe?"*

"Stay out of my head."

She remained aloft, listening to their conversation, keeping watch over Jorn where he sat in the opening of the cave by the fire.

The hunter nodded to the fire. "Mind if I share the cave today? I'd planned to stay the night and smoke some meat."

Jorn skinned and cleaned the rabbit as he spoke. "I'll only be here long enough to cook something to eat. Then the cave is all yours."

The hunter dropped the deer on the ground by the fire. "Where are you headed?"

"Home." Jorn rigged some forked branches and created a spit for the rabbit.

"Is that far from here?" The hunter crouched by the deer, taking out his dagger.

"A little way."

Worried by the way he kept avoiding the other hunter's questions, Morgane asked him, *"Is something wrong?"*

Jorn glanced up before returning his attention to the rabbit he cooked over the fire. *"You can hear us?"*

She wasn't able to prevent him from hearing her mental laughter. *"I'm a dragon. We have really good hearing."* And she wasn't that far away.

Again he looked up, slowly turning his head. *"Where are you?"*

"To your left. I'm staying out of sight of your friend."

"That hasn't been decided yet." Jorn glanced at the other hunter who continued to skin the deer, his back to Morgane.

"Should I collect you?"

"Do you want to get me killed?"

"Just so we're clear. It's not you I'm worried about. It's your sister and cousin."

"Why?"

She had no idea how to answer him. Really had no idea how the three of them had become friends. It had just happened. They'd been tracking the same rabbit. She'd been as startled as they had been when she'd come across the two young girls. She'd been warned by Gilda so many times that the hunters killed any dragon they came across. To take to the skies if she should see one. Yet the two girls had seemed scared of her. It had surprised her when Elin had asked if she planned to eat them, Anja trying to hush her. Somehow one question had led to another on both sides until the rabbit had been forgotten and they'd spent the rest of the afternoon trying to sate their curiosity. That afternoon had been followed by others until the three of them were sneaking away and meeting every chance they could.

"Morgane? Are you still there?"

"I'm here."

"You didn't answer my question."

"I don't plan to. Ask your sister if you want to know anything." She didn't want to get either of her friends in any more trouble than it sounded like they already were in. *"Is she really going to be ostracised?"*

"Would that matter to you?"

She didn't hesitate to answer. *"Yes."*

"Then stay away from her. Tell her you no longer wish to see her."

The thought of never seeing Elin or Anja again hit her like a physical blow. She tried to contain the feeling, wanting to keep it from leaking through to Jorn.

"What happened? Were you attacked?"

She tried to steady her emotions. Tried to remind herself she at least had Gwynham. But it wasn't the same. There were things she could share with Elin and Anja that she couldn't share with her brother. And it wasn't because she wasn't a proper dragon like her mother had told her more than once. She wasn't a hunter. Wasn't interested in being one. But that didn't mean she had to hate them. That she couldn't be friends with them. Although technically neither of her friends were hunters. Only villagers. For now. Soon Elin would be a hunter. If she wasn't thrown out of the village.

Jorn cut strips of meat from the rabbit he left on the spit above the fire. He blew on them to cool them down quicker. *"Morgane? Were you attacked?"*

She breathed in deeply, wishing she could breathe out flames. *"I have to see them one more time. They wouldn't believe a message from you."* Scanning the clearing, she chose a location that would be out of the other hunter's sight and landed, shapeshifting to slip in amongst the trees. She sank to the ground, leaning against the trunk of a tree and drawing her knees up to wrap her arms around them. It didn't help the pain.

"What happened? I know something did. What aren't you telling me?"

"You're rather dense, aren't you?"

"What?"

She tightened her arms around her legs. *"Forget it."* She didn't bother keeping the bitterness from her thoughts. When he didn't immediately answer, she thought he'd remain silent.

"*You care about them. Elin and Anja. They're more than friends.*"

Surprise and another emotion she couldn't figure out had accompanied his statement. She wanted to ask him what it was, but he was nothing like Elin and Anja. There'd been times when the two had wished she was a sister and she'd echoed their wish, saying that whichever one gained a sister would also gain a brother. Yet each time she'd made that wish, she'd always wanted them to be a dragon like her. "*They're the family of my heart.*" She repeated the words her friends had often spoken to her, feeling the shock from him that echoed through their link.

"*They said that to you?*"

"*Yes.*"

"*Did they ever…*" His thoughts trailed off.

She was tempted to leave him wondering, but worried it would get her friends in more trouble. "*We talked about the ceremony to accept someone into your family, but never performed it.*" When they'd told her it'd make her one of them, she'd worried it might make her less of a dragon. The wave of relief she felt from him at her words nearly overwhelmed her pain.

"*Why are you still here?*"

"*I will escort you home.*"

"*It isn't like you can fly from here. Not with this hunter to see. These are my forests. I've roamed them since the day I could walk. I'm more than capable of finding my way home."*

"There's another clearing not far from here. A smaller one. I can fly you to a clearing closer to home from there."

"Then we're done and I need never see you again."

Once again she fought against the pain that washed over her, somehow managing to keep it from him. It wasn't that she wanted to see him again, it was his and the rest of the villagers' belief that she wasn't worth knowing. A belief that would keep her apart from her friends. *"I can't imagine why we should meet again."*

"And tomorrow you'll tell my sister you no longer want to see her. And Anja."

"Not tomorrow."

"And not the day after that? Nor day after that one? So tell me, will the day ever come for you to tell them goodbye?"

"Not tomorrow. Any other day than tomorrow."

"What's so special about tomorrow?"

She could hear the demand in his thoughts, threaded through with anger. She wanted to protest she hadn't been lying to him. *"It's the celebration of my birth."*

There was a lengthy silence before Jorn commented. *"The day after then."*

She couldn't answer immediately. *"The day after."*

Silence settled between them, neither of them talking to each other. If it wasn't that she could sense Jorn, she would have thought he'd left the area. Only the crackle of the fire and the scent of cooking meat let her know someone was nearby. Hunters were disconcertingly silent. Nothing like the savages you could hear coming.

"Are you ready?"

Not having expected the comment, it took her a moment to answer. *"Yes. I'll meet up with you once you're amongst the trees."* She skirted the clearing as she listened to Jorn speak to the other hunter.

"The fire and campsite are all yours."

"Thank you." The hunter paused a moment. "Be careful on your journey. I caught a glimpse of a dragon in the sky earlier."

"Thank you for your warning. May your rest go undisturbed."

Shock arrowed through her. He'd seen her? Had he seen Jorn riding on her back? She hoped not. After all this effort, she didn't want to get him killed. Villagers assumed those that were associated with dragons were traitors. She hadn't even known the villagers had found out Elin and Anja knew her. It was a wonder they hadn't sent hunters to track her down. Remaining as quiet as possible she hurried through the forest so she could meet up with Jorn. She wanted to search the hunter's mind to learn if he'd seen them, but she wasn't that good at it yet. Would it be worse for him to know she'd remained in the area? Or better to confirm whether or not he'd seen Jorn?

She was so busy trying to figure out what to do, she nearly walked into Jorn, who was invisible. She sidestepped him at the last moment.

He appeared beside her, continuing to walk through the forest. "How did you know I was there?"

Keeping up with him, she debated telling him. He already knew far too much for someone who didn't like dragons.

"I thought I hid my scent and sounds. What gave me away? Can dragons find us when we're hidden?"

An image of Elin came to mind and she sighed heavily. "Don't ever let a dragon take your blood." Very few of those who'd come to this world had the ability, but it would be better if he was wary of all dragons.

"You didn't want to tell me that, so why did you?"

She glanced at him. "Elin."

"How could I forget? My sister is the only reason you're keeping me alive."

"And your cousin." She glanced at him again. "Were you expecting another reason?"

He didn't answer immediately. "I feel like I should owe you."

"Don't. If I did it for you, then you would. But I didn't."

"So my sister owes you?" he demanded.

"Would you expect her to owe you if you helped her?"

"No."

"Exactly." She glanced at him several times when he fell silent, wondering what he was thinking. Neither talked as they traipsed through the forest, eventually reaching the next clearing. She focused on the area, breathing deep and listening carefully. The wildlife seemed to be going about their normal business, none of them scurrying out of the way. She stepped out from the treeline and into the open. Nothing. Wanting to get out of the open, she shapeshifted, holding her wing out of the way so Jorn could clamber onto her back. The moment he was in place, she took to the sky heading in the direction of his village. The silence between them felt strange, but she had no reason to break it. Wings pumping, she headed high above the trees, not wanting to risk catching the attention of any of the hunters wandering the forest.

Chapter Four

It was well after the middle of the day when Morgane landed in a clearing closer to the village. Once Jorn was off her back, she became human again.

"I can find my own way from here."

She didn't comment, watching him vanish, sensing as he walked away. She waited until he was a good distance before she followed, wanting to make sure he arrived home safely. She wasn't about to follow him all the way to the village. She wasn't crazy.

"Why are you following me? I told you to go home."

His voice in her head interrupted her thoughts, startling her. *"You can hear me?"*

"No. I marked your signature."

"Signature?" She winced, not having meant to give away that she didn't know what he was talking about.

"So there were some things they didn't tell you."

She walked towards him, sensing he'd stopped

walking. *"I'd never use what they taught me against someone they cared about."*

He appeared in front of her, speaking aloud this time. "But you'd use it against someone they don't care about?"

She looked past him. "I'm late. I told my brother I'd be home before the middle of the day. Surely someone must be missing you by now."

He shrugged. "I sent the hunters, that were with me, back to the village with the deer we killed rather than risk them catching Elin with you." He paused a moment. "If you're running late, why are you still here?" He captured a lock of her hair. "It's not like any hunter could miss spotting you."

She tugged her hair from his fingers. "If you're sure you're close enough to home." She took a step back.

He nodded and started to turn away, facing her again. "The day after?"

She wanted to disagree, but she wouldn't allow Elin or Anja to be ostracised from their village. Both wanted to become hunters. Even without magic, Anja could become one if someone was willing to be her hunting companion. Elin had promised that if she passed the ceremony, she'd be Anja's companion. "The next day." Spinning, she raced through the forest towards the clearing, ignoring Jorn's voice in her head.

"Answer me, Morgane. What is wrong?"

When she sensed him move towards her, she finally answered. *"I'm late. Go home."*

"You won't forget."

She stumbled into the clearing, shapeshifting and taking to the sky. *"How can I?"* She sensed him moving towards the village so she headed for the castle. She doubted she'd be able to sneak in with how late she was. Her brother was probably wondering what had happened to her. She mentally searched ahead, trying to contact him. Unable to find him that way she used his blood to sense where he was, locating him in his room. She focused on the location, trying to figure out why her sense of him was less than usual.

Before she could try sensing for him elsewhere, she landed on the battlements, glancing at the patrolling warriors. They would let her mother know she'd returned. Striding inside, she headed towards her brother's room. Flinging the door open, she frowned. The room was empty, yet she could sense him in here. She moved further into the room. The timber floor gleamed like it had been freshly washed. She stopped, staring at the bed, the dark timber looking like it had been recently cleaned and the bedding having been changed. He was under the bed? A sound had her spinning towards the door.

The petite woman in the doorway had eyes almost gold in colour, anger clearly visible in them, her rich brown hair filled with gold highlights. "We thought you'd been lost to us. Gwynham told me you'd be back this morning. Yet when we searched for you, we couldn't sense you anywhere. Where have you been?"

"Mother–"

Brigitte interrupted her. "Where have you been?" She spoke each word slowly and carefully, a sharpness to them.

"Hunting." Her fingers brushed across the quiver at her side, her expression blank as she forced herself to remain where she was and not retreat. She would have preferred to change into something dry rather than remain in her damp gear.

Brigitte's lips curled in distaste. "We are warriors, not hunters. You should carry your sword at your side. Not a bow at your back. You've always been a disappointment to me. Are you trying to shame me? Start acting like a dragon. Not a hunter."

Morgane pressed her lips together on the words she wanted to speak. They never made any difference to her mother's frequent complaints. She was a dragon. A Gold dragon. Not wanting to carry a sword and preferring to hunt with a bow didn't make her any less of a dragon.

"We thought you dead. Yet here you are." Brigitte gestured towards her with a graceful movement of her hand. "Alive."

Morgane kept her breathing even, pushing her emotions down. "Is that disappointing too?"

"I had plans this morning that you ruined."

She held the relief she felt in check, not ready to give into it yet. That might involve letting her guard down. "Plans?"

"Nevermind." Brigitte made a sweeping motion with her hand. "To show you I'm not angry, I have a gift for you." She took a hinged bracelet from a pocket of her dress, holding it out. It was a dull silver, almost grey in colour. "Come closer. Surely you wouldn't reject a gift from me."

She wanted to point out that her mother was clearly angry. It would only make things worse. "No, Mother." She held out her left hand, placing it in her mother's. She needed to find Gwynham so she could learn what he'd told their mother about her being away. If he was under the bed, he was probably waiting for their mother to leave the room before he came out. Yet her sense of him should have been stronger if that was where he was hiding.

Brigitte snapped the bracelet closed around her wrist, raising it to her lips, tilting her head forward to press them against the join of the metal, murmuring softly against it. Smiling, Brigitte let her go. "You will stay close to home. No more wandering." There was a glitter of triumph in Brigitte's eyes. "It's no longer safe for you out there." She swept out of the room.

Morgane stood where she was, her hand held out as it sank in what her mother had done. Her gaze remained fixed on the bracelet, snug around her wrist. It was made from a mixture of metals, including the one that was used to chain up dragons and prevent them from becoming human or using their abilities. This one had been made with the help of the hunters who'd joined her mother. Created to keep a dragon in human form and reduce the power of their abilities. It was the first time she'd seen the metal. Anger rushed through her when it wouldn't open. When had they perfected the metal? When had they turned it into jewellery? Had this been her mother's plan all along? And how much had they made? Who else did her mother plan to use it on?

Was this why she couldn't sense Gwynham properly before?

"I'm too late. Oh, my hatchling. I'm too late."

Morgane raised her gaze to the woman in the doorway. The curvaceous woman had black hair plaited back from her face. "Gilda, I can't find Gwynham." She half turned towards the bed. "Unless-" Surely he wouldn't have remained hidden once their mother had left the room.

Gilda hurried to her, grabbing her hand and tugging her further away from the bed. "No. Come away."

"What happened?" She met Gilda's gaze, seeing the fear and worry in the green eyes. "Gilda?" She tugged her hand from Gilda's light grip. "Where's Gwynham?"

Gilda continued to slowly shake her head.

Morgane backed away from her. "Tell me where he is."

"She was in such a rage when you didn't return. I never would have expected it of her. This place, it's been terrible for her. Changed her from the hatchling I raised. Her father should never have brought her here. Should never have cloistered her away in his home and not prevented her from hunting a Pliethin so she could access her full power as a gold."

She didn't need to hear this old story again. All she needed to know was where her brother was. "Gilda, where is he?" She backed away, taking a step closer to the bed. "Where is my brother?"

"She said there were two of you. And she only needed one. What good was two when she needed the heart of a gold?"

The words struck her more harshly than Jorn's had earlier. "No." The word was little more than an expulsion of air. Spinning, she hurried to the bed, dropping to her knees to look under it. There was a splatter of blood on the floorboards. She pressed a hand against it. The blood was dry. She shrugged Gilda's hands from her shoulders.

"She wouldn't listen. I told her there was no reason the heart of a Gold would work any better than the heart of a common dragon in this world. But she wouldn't listen. Kept saying she could see age marks on her face and she wouldn't have it. That she would live long enough to find her own way home. That obviously she couldn't rely on others to save her."

Rising to her feet, Morgane grabbed hold of Gilda's hands. "Where is Gwynham?" She needed to see him. Needed to know how badly he'd been injured. Surely they hadn't taken his heart. He must have escaped. He was a great warrior and had never set aside his sword like she'd done.

Gilda opened her mouth several times, ending up shaking her head instead of speaking.

"If you won't answer me, then help me take this off." She let go of one of Gilda's hands to raise her wrist to eye level. "Help me get rid of it."

"I don't know what word she would have used to seal it."

Morgane wanted to roar. But all she'd be capable of doing in this form was scream. That wasn't good enough. "You've known her for her entire life."

"There were the decades I spent raising her younger siblings. The time during which she met your father. I'm so sorry. I tried to stop her. And I tried to be here when you arrived. I failed both of you today." Gilda's voice broke.

"Then tell me where Gwynham is. Did he escape?"

"Telling you won't help. Trust me on this. It won't help. No one can help him now."

The words cut deep and again she wanted to roar. "When?" She tried to swallow down the lump in her throat. She shouldn't be feeling this pain. Was everyone right? If she truly was a dragon, she should feel only anger and a need for revenge. "When did it happen?"

"The middle of the day, when no one could find you."

She closed her eyes, swaying on her feet. It was her fault. If only she hadn't tried to save Elin's brother. "I should have been here."

"Then it would have been you who would have taken his place. The four of you are… were the only golds left in this world. She wasn't about to do anything to Dorran. She's already planning children with him now they know the heart of a Gold works. Both of them are hoping for more Golds."

Shock spiralled through her as she realised their plan. A plan they'd already begun. "They would eat the hearts of their children to extend their lives?" What would they do to the children that weren't Gold? Only one of Dorran's parents had been Gold so it wasn't a guarantee that all his offspring would be born Gold.

Gilda nodded once, unable to meet her gaze. "They have already. Or at least your mother has."

Nausea struck at the thought of Brigitte consuming Gwynham's heart. Of deliberately killing him for his heart. "No." Shaking her head, she backed away from Gilda until she ran into the wall. "No."

"Survival of the fittest."

Gilda's soft words stabbed at her with reminders of

all the pain she'd endured because of them. She forced the emotions away, struggling to remain standing. She was a dragon. Empathy and pain didn't make her weak. "I need to see him." Her voice was more commanding than she'd expected it to be. Especially with how she felt crumpled and torn inside. She couldn't be the only dragon who'd ever felt this way. Maybe it was only that other dragons were better at hiding their pain.

"You don't want to see him. You don't want to remember him like that. Remember him as he was."

Chapter Five

A rush of anger forced the pain aside, burning through Morgane. This was how a dragon should feel. Her body felt stronger and her hands curled into fists. For a moment she thought she sensed her brother amongst the outbuildings. Then it was gone. The anger ebbed and she was struck anew by his death. She couldn't help looking in the direction of the outbuildings, even though it was impossible to see them through the thick walls of the castle.

Gilda came forward and took hold of her hands, uncurling her fingers. "No. You don't want to see him."

She stared at Gilda for a moment. He was in that direction? How had she sensed him? If she could do it once surely she could do it again. Breaking free from Gilda's grip, she raced from the room, the soft soles of her leather boots barely making a sound. Elin and Anja would be proud of how softly she ran. The thought of the two of them brought a fresh wave of pain. How could she survive losing everyone in a single day? She stumbled as the pain swamped her.

Pushing the pain aside, she forced herself to run faster, ignoring Gilda who called after her. She had to see Gwynham. Had to know for certain what had happened to him. There was a small part of her that couldn't believe he was dead. That hoped he'd somehow escaped.

She sidestepped one of the servants and nearly ran into a warrior. Ignoring the glare he sent her way, she ran down the stairs that led to the back of the castle and outside. When she stepped outside, she felt a slight tug in the direction of the outbuildings. There was a mixture of storage sheds, stables, workshops and preparation areas for various tasks.

She slowed to a walk, trying to figure out where he was. Nothing. She tugged at the bracelet on her wrist. There had to be a way to get rid of it. Finding her brother had always been the simplest of things to do. Now she struggled to find a sense of his blood at all. Wandering through the outbuildings, she peered inside some of them. It wasn't until she was approaching the slaughterhouse that she could sense his blood. She faced the door, staring at the timber planks. They'd brought him here like a beast to be slaughtered? Once again the pain was swamped by anger and she pushed the door open to stalk inside. The anger evaporated as quickly as it had come and she staggered to the solid wooden worktable in the middle of the dirt floor building.

"No." The word was drawn from her, little more than a moan. This wasn't Gwynham. She slowly shook her head. This wasn't her brother.

"Morgane." Gilda hurried to her side, holding up an oil lamp, banishing the shadows in the building.

She drew in a sharp breath when the lamp highlighted her brother's sightless, pale blue eyes. "Gwynham." She sank her fingers into his white blond hair that was the same length as hers. The strands were streaked with blood. Dried blood. She hadn't been here when he'd needed her. They'd always been there for each other.

"Come out of here, Morgane," Gilda said softly.

Her gaze remained fixed on her brother. His shirt was ripped and torn, as was his chest. She breathed in deeply, the scent of blood overpowering. It reminded her of the deer the hunter had dropped on the ground by the fire pit. Another wave of anger struck her and she tightened her fingers in her brother's hair. "Did they eat all of it?" When Gilda didn't answer, she reached for the cavity of Gwynham's chest.

Gilda grabbed hold of her wrist, trying to draw her hand back from Gwynham. "Don't. It's not in there."

She needed to find out for herself. She tugged her hand from Gilda's grip and plunged it inside her brother's chest. The heart was gone. She wiped her hand on her brother's trousers, turning to face Gilda, anger again rushing through her. "Did they eat all of it?"

Gilda took a step away from her, shaking her head.

She didn't bother reassuring Gilda that she wouldn't hurt her. Right this moment, she wasn't certain what she'd do. Her hands tightened into fists. "Where is the rest of his heart?"

Gilda glanced over her shoulder before meeting Morgane's gaze again. "She put it in a small timber box and sent two warriors north with it. I don't know where she told them to take it, but I can only assume they continued north into the high mountains where the snow is on the ground year round."

"Why didn't he-" She broke off as she realised he was in human form. She spun to face him, lifting his wrist. There was a familiar bracelet wrapped around it. One identical to hers. No wonder he hadn't been able to take flight. An image of her brother in dragon form filled her mind. A large silver creature with gold flecks scattered across his scales and blue eyes shot through with gold.

Gilda came close, resting a hand on Morgane's shoulder. "You can do nothing for him now. Come away before someone finds you in here. Don't let her find out how much this has hurt you."

Again she spun to face Gilda. "There is something I can do for him." She reached for his hand, holding it tightly. Unlike previous times, no one squeezed her hand in answer. "I can avenge him."

"You don't have it in you. You could never end your mother's life. You haven't been raised amongst dragons your own age. Have spent more time with humans than your own kind."

The words were too close to the accusations that had already been thrown at her today. "And whose fault is that? My-" She broke off, unable to say the words 'my mother'. "Brigitte wouldn't allow us to mix with the children of common warriors." Not that many had been born during the years they'd lived in this world. "And she certainly wouldn't let us mix with the half-dragons or with the children of humans."

"Morgane-"

"No. I don't want to hear it. I might not be able to

end her life, but I can end Dorran's and I will stop her from consuming another piece of my brother's heart." It wasn't much and she almost hated herself for not being able to avenge him like he deserved.

"You can do nothing as a human. You don't know what it's like to be so powerless amongst those with power greater than you can imagine."

"You think I don't know what it's like to be powerless?" Morgane demanded. "I have spent my entire life in Mothe... Brigitte's control." She gestured towards Gwynham. "Both of us have." She'd had enough. No more. "I will do whatever it takes to escape her control." She raised her chin. "Even if it means joining my brother."

"You can't-"

Again she interrupted Gilda. "Will you help me? Or do I need to do this alone?"

Gilda placed the lamp beside Gwynham then threw her arms around Morgane. "Oh, my hatchling. Don't ask me to help you to your death. I couldn't stand to lose both of you."

Morgane wrapped her arms around Gilda. "Then help me live. Do you think I'll be safe when they run out of Gwynham's heart to keep them young? It won't take Brigitte long to eat the last of it if all it takes are a few barely noticeable lines on her face to have her wanting more. I'm not about to sit around here with a death sentence hanging over my head." Not that she had anywhere else to go. She thought of Elin and Anja. The villagers would never let her stay with either of them.

"Tell me you at least have a plan," Gilda begged.

Letting go of Gilda, her gaze was drawn to Gwynham. She was a dragon. No matter how often Brigitte told her she wasn't. And dragons lived to hatch plans. Cunning, devious plans. Stepping close to her brother, she drew a dagger and cut a lock of bloodstained hair. After drawing out the sodden scarf, letting it fall to the floor, she slipped it inside the damp belt pouch at her left hip. Sheathing the dagger, she faced Gilda. "I have a plan." It was more of a desired outcome, but she'd turn it into a plan. "Fetch me a length of cloth I can wrap Gwynham in. I can't leave him here to be processed for others to consume. Or for his skin to be used to make dragon-leather clothes."

"What are you going to do with him?" Gilda asked.

Morgane blew out the lamp and set it on the ground beside the door. "Hurry. Brigitte will expect us to dine with her tonight." That didn't give her much time to get everything done.

Gilda stared at her a moment longer before she nodded once and hurried away.

With one last look at her brother, Morgane stepped outside and closed the door. She pushed all thoughts of Gwynham from her mind. It allowed thoughts of Elin and Anja to creep in. She couldn't think of them either. Thoughts of Jorn entered her mind. Had he made it back safely? At least thoughts of him didn't fill her with pain.

She continued to think about him as she searched for a hiding place amongst the outbuildings for her brother. He wasn't bad looking for a human. And if he'd been the one to have taken down the deer alone, he was a good hunter too. A smile fleetingly appeared. He'd certainly taken out his share of the savages. Nor had he panicked when she'd grabbed hold of him and taken him into the air. He was as fearless as his sister. Not that it mattered. They could never be friends.

She frowned, wondering why that thought bothered her. Surely she wasn't so desperate for company she'd befriend anyone she stumbled across. A smile partly formed as she recalled his dry tone. 'It would involve admitting you might be wrong.' The smile faded and she slowly shook her head. He had no idea what it was like to be a dragon. Being wrong was perilous and could lead to your death. She tried not to think of Gwynham. But she couldn't stop the image of him lying on the timber worktable from invading her mind. She'd obviously made the wrong decision today. She should have been here so they could have faced Brigitte and her warriors together. Not that it would have changed much, but at least he wouldn't have died alone.

Finding a hiding place behind a stack of timber, she returned to the slaughterhouse. Gilda had wrapped Gwynham in a length of cloth, stitching it closed along the front. She picked up her brother and sent Gilda ahead to keep an eye out for anyone who might stop her. Once her brother was hidden, she returned to the castle and gathered together some items she put in a rucksack. She hid it, along with her longbow and quiver, beside her brother.

She barely had enough time to wash and dress in a formal gown and cloth slippers so she could dine with Brigitte, setting her boots and belt pouch by the fireplace in her bedroom to finish drying. The layers of petticoats under the floor length skirt felt odd after a week in dragon-leather trousers. Reaching the hall, she slowed her steps as her gaze scanned the candlelit room.

Brigitte was at the head of the table, Dorran on

her right, the chair at her left empty. Various warriors were seated around the table, a seat towards the end left free for Gilda. Morgane tried not to focus on the warrior who sat on the seat to the left of the one that remained empty for her. Gwynham had taken turns sharing it with her, the two of them alternating between which one of them sat beside Brigitte. Seeing another in the seat had her fighting to keep the pain at bay. She managed to keep her face expressionless, her gaze drawn to Brigitte who smiled at Dorran.

Her hands curled into fists and her fingernails dug into her flesh. When Brigitte looked in her direction, she forced her hands to relax, returning the smile, as she walked towards the table. Like the smile directed at her, there was no warmth in hers. When Brigitte's smile faltered for the tiniest bit, her own widened. Brigitte's smile faded, replaced by a look of warning.

Morgane pulled out the timber chair and sat at the table. Before this ended, she'd make sure Brigitte had more than the tiniest moment of concern. She lifted the goblet in front of her, raising it to her lips. At the last moment, she realised it could be poisoned and dampened her lips with it rather than drink it. She placed it on the table, raising the linen cloth to her lips, dabbing at them before spreading it across her lap. "Have you anything planned to celebrate the day of my birth tomorrow?"

Brigitte raised her own goblet, tilting it towards Morgane with a single nod of the head before taking a sip. "My warriors rounded up some villagers today. We'll see how they do barehanded against a dragon tomorrow." She took another sip from the goblet she continued to hold. "It should be entertaining." A smile formed, a look of triumph glittering in her eyes.

Morgane managed to keep her expression neutral, all the while wanting to seek out the humans and make sure she knew none of them. Was this a punishment for her? Had Brigitte learned who she'd been with the past week? And when had the villagers been rounded up? This morning? Or after Elin and Anja had returned home.

Placing the goblet on the table, Brigitte glanced at the servant standing at her shoulder. "Why have we not been served?"

The servant clapped his hands together loudly and the hall was filled by humans carrying plates of steaming food. One was placed in front of Brigitte first, followed by Dorran and then Morgane.

Chapter Six

Reaching for her goblet, Morgane deliberately knocked it over in a manner to make it look accidental. The wine flooded her plate and splashed onto her gown, soaking through the cloth she'd placed across her lap. She leapt back from the table, knocking over her chair, the saturated cloth landing on the floor. She held her hands out, away from her gown as she looked down at it. "I need to change."

Gilda rose from where she sat towards the other end of the table.

Morgane waved her back into her seat. "I'm perfectly capable of tending to myself." She gave Brigitte a nod. "I'll return once I've cleaned myself and changed my gown."

Brigitte gave the mess on the table a distasteful look before focusing her attention on Morgane. "I will not hold the meal for you. Take too long and you'll go without."

Morgane, who'd started to turn away, faced Brigitte again. "I understand." She gave Brigitte another nod before she strode from the hall. She stepped to the side to avoid one of the servants, snatching a slice of meat from the plate they carried. As soon as she was out of hearing, she ran to her room and slipped out of her dress and petticoats, leaving them in a puddle on the floor. Only the top layers had been soaked.

She changed into a dragon-leather shirt and trousers and pulled on her now dry boots. After plaiting back her hair, and coiling it around her head, she wrapped her head in a dragon-leather scarf to hide the brightness of her hair. Buckling her belt, she headed outside to the stone building the captured humans were kept in before they were convinced of the benefits of becoming servants to Brigitte. She wasn't about to let Brigitte kill them to make a point for her. Surely she wouldn't know any of them. Brigitte could barely tell the humans that served her apart from one another. There was no way she'd be able to recognise Elin or Anja to have her warriors take them captive.

Morgane was almost at the building, slipping

through the shadows of the night, when she sensed a familiar villager. Anja! What was she doing here? Her friend couldn't fight against a dragon. She didn't have the magic needed to survive. A scan of the area showed it was empty. Like she'd expected, nearly everyone was inside eating. There'd be a few patrolling the battlements, but that would be it.

Hurrying towards the building, she mentally tried to speak to Anja. She nearly growled in frustration, managing to remain silent instead. Pressing herself against the stone wall, she tried to sense where her friend was. On the far side of the building. She couldn't prevent a sigh from escaping. Eventually, Brigitte would send someone to look for her. She had to be as far from here as possible by then.

There was nothing deadening Brigitte's dragon abilities and Brigitte would be able to sense where she was if she didn't get out of here. It'd take her a lot longer to cover the ground on foot than it would when she was able to fly. Pressing against the wall on the far side of the building, she mentally reached for Anja again. It was an effort, but she made contact.

"Morgane? Where are you?" Anja asked.

"The wall opposite the door. Come close to it." She smiled when the familiar link became easier to use. *"What happened?"*

"We have a traitor in the village. The eight of us in here have either no magic or as good as none. Did you come for me?"

She had no idea what to tell Anja. *"Pay attention. You'll have to move quickly. Memorise these directions."* She showed Anja image after image, interrupting her friend's questions. *"Think you can remember that path through the castle grounds?"*

"Aren't you coming with us?" Anja waited for a reply. *"Morgane?"*

"She killed Gwynham."

"Someone killed your brother?"

"Yes."

"Who."

"I'll meet you at the door." She moved away from Anja, breaking the link, not wanting to answer the question her friend had asked her. How could she explain that her own mother had killed one of her children and planned to kill more? As many as it took to keep her from aging. Reaching the door, she slid the bar back and swung it open, sensing Anja on the other side.

"Mor-"

"Shh." She sidestepped her friend's attempt at an

embrace. *"You have to leave. All of you. They'll notice me missing at any moment."*

Anja captured her hand. *"Come with us."*

"I can't." She glanced at the humans crowding behind Anja. There were only two people in the village who'd welcome her. The rest would want her dead. *"Go. Please."*

Anja managed to throw her arms around Morgane. *"Come see us tomorrow. In the usual place."*

She returned the embrace. There wasn't time now to tell Anja she was leaving the region. *"All right."* She pulled away from her friend. *"Go before it's too late."*

Anja nodded, glancing over her shoulder to the seven humans with her. Again she nodded and they followed her through the buildings, moonlight showing the way through the shadows.

Morgane watched them longer than she should, turning away and running to where she'd left her brother and her gear. Once her quiver and rucksack were in place she slipped an arm and her head through the longbow. There wasn't enough in the rucksack to prevent the bow from sitting across her back. A spare set of dragon-leather clothes, a cloak, flint and steel and some dried food. She could live off the land. Had done so the past week. Maybe she was more of a hunter than a dragon. Anger rushed through her. No. Brigitte was wrong. Being able to hunt with a bow didn't make her any less of a dragon. Her gaze was drawn to the bracelet. Once she found a way to remove it, she'd once more be able to shapeshift into her true form.

Taking a deep breath, she hoisted the cloth wrapped body of her brother into her arms. He was heavier than he would normally be for her. The bracelet was obviously affecting more than her ability to sense where familiar people were and to mind talk. What other dragon abilities had it decreased? Speed? Stamina? Hearing?

Remaining in the shadows, she hurried towards an exit at the rear of the castle. There was no way she could leave by the front. She'd be a lot more noticeable, than the humans, while carrying her brother. But she wasn't about to leave him behind.

A sound drew her attention and she turned to see a warrior. It would be impossible to avoid him. A handful more steps and he'd spot her. In one fluid motion, she lowered her brother and grabbed her bow, putting an arrow to it and drawing it back. Her gaze scanned the ground and she saw a pebble, kicking it off to the right, letting go of the string when the warrior's attention was caught by the pebble skittering across the ground. The arrow took him in the throat and he staggered backwards, the second arrow piercing his heart.

Not waiting to see if he was dying, she slung her bow across her back and gathered up her brother, holding him close as she hurried towards the exit. Heart racing, she strained to catch every sound, regularly breathing in deep to sift through the nearby scents. She had no idea if she was catching all of them, could only hope she made it out alive. And that the humans did too. The thought had no sooner formed when a shout went up from the front of the castle.

Anja! Not Anja. Desperation clawed through her. Ahead was a pond the castle servants brought the washing to, behind was the castle and Anja, shouts continuing to ring out. Past the pond was the forest and safety. She glanced over her shoulder. She couldn't leave Anja behind. Nor could she desert her brother for them to find. She had to hide him. Her gaze was drawn to the pond. Facing forward, she entered the water and tossed him into a deep section, her heart sinking with him, the cold water making her shiver. She'd return for him once Anja was safe.

Turning towards the castle, she waded back to shore, racing around the outside of the castle wall to where the commotion was coming from. Rounding the corner, she spotted a warrior slam into Anja, knocking her friend to the ground. He drew a sword, swinging it back. All around were other warriors and humans, blood staining the ground.

Anger and fear exploded inside her as she automatically grabbed her bow and an arrow, aiming at the warrior's heart. The arrow pierced his back as she mentally screamed for Anja to run, wishing Elin was here to help. Even Jorn would be better than nothing right now. She fired an arrow at another warrior that turned to attack Anja.

"Morgane?"

She faltered, the next arrow missing its target. *"Jorn?"* There was nothing. She'd imagined it.

She fired arrow after arrow at the warriors, many of the arrows being plucked from the air and tossed back at her. She dodged each of them, grabbing some of them and returning them to her quiver. Two warriors ran towards her. There was no way she could escape them. An arrow pierced one, coming from the right and the direction of the forest. The second warrior turned towards the forest. That was his mistake. She shot him through the neck. The second arrow went through his heart when he turned towards her, ripping the arrow from his neck. His knees hit the ground and she fired another arrow into him. He toppled backwards, becoming a dragon as he hit the ground.

"Morgane!" Anja stood at the edge of the forest. "Run." She gestured wildly towards the castle, disappearing when a hand dragged her amongst the trees.

Morgane turned slightly, barely keeping her expression blank when she saw the warriors coming out of the castle entrance. There was no way she could take on that many. A quick check of the ground in front of the castle showed only three humans had been killed. The other bodies were the warriors she'd taken out, probably dead since all were now in dragon form. None of the residents of the castle were going to be happy about the deaths. She did as Anja had ordered and ran.

She pushed herself as hard as she could, but it didn't feel like she could go as fast as usual. She'd nearly reached the treeline when an impact sent her sprawling across the ground. This close she couldn't miss sensing Jorn. There was a thud in a tree ahead of her. The hunters who'd turned traitor against their own people to join Brigitte must have joined the warriors in coming after her.

"Why can't I talk to you? In your mind, like earlier." Jorn's voice was against her ear and his hand wrapped around her wrist as he dragged her to her feet, becoming invisible once it was only his hand in contact with her.

"Long story." And it certainly wasn't one she wanted to tell him. She ran towards the forest, her gaze momentarily resting on the arrow embedded in the tree. As she slipped into the forest, she nodded towards the arrow. "Happy? Looks like we're even now."

"Not even close." Jorn let go of her, but continued to run at her side.

"Morgane, over here." Anja stepped into a splash of moonlight filtered through the leaves of the trees.

Morgane raced to her friend's side, grabbing hold of her arms. "Are you unharmed?"

Anja nodded. "Mostly."

Morgane glanced around. "Did any others escape?"

Jorn became visible and dragged Morgane away from Anja. "The trees won't stop them. They'll gather more and come after us. We have to return to the village."

Morgane nodded, turning to Anja. "Tell Elin-" She broke off at the sharp pain that raced through her. She tried again. "I have to leave the area."

"When will you be back?" Anja asked.

Jorn slung his bow onto his back, grabbing both

their arms and tugging them further into the forest. "There isn't time for this."

"Where are you going?" Anja demanded.

She thought of what Gilda had said, trying to see Anja on the other side of Jorn who continued to tug them further into the forest. "North."

"Are you crazy?" Anja demanded. "The creatures of nightmares live there."

"You're both crazy." Jorn let go of Morgane. "Go before you're caught." He tugged Anja further into the forest. "Everyone's been looking for you, Anja. And the others. The forest is crawling with hunters tonight."

Morgane slowed to a stop, catching glimpses of Anja and Jorn as they moved further away. It seemed like nowhere was safe for her tonight. She took a step towards the right, away from the direction of the village, light bursting in front of her.

A hunter appeared before her, a ball of light in his hand. "Dragon." He said the word like it was a curse.

Chapter Seven

Morgane turned away, her attempt at escape halted by three other hunters appearing around her. There was enough light she could see Jorn struggling to keep Anja from her, his hand clamped over her mouth. She wanted to tell her friend to run, to forget about her, but she couldn't. The bracelet prevented her from doing so.

"Nothing to say for yourself, Dragon?"

She spun to face the hunter who'd first appeared in front of her. "Would anything I say make a difference?"

The hunter opened his mouth to speak.

Jorn interrupted, continuing to hold Anja. "We need to bring her back to the village. We need to ask her why she set our people free."

"What does it matter?" a hunter behind Morgane demanded.

She remained facing the hunter who'd first appeared. She couldn't bear the thought of Elin and Anja being killed. Yet there was little she could do to protect them. An image of her brother filled her mind. She hadn't even been able to protect him. "They will live forever."

"Who will live forever?" the first hunter demanded.

"Forget about talking to her, Tarben. All she deserves is death. It's all any of them deserve," the same hunter behind Morgane said. "Look at what they've done to our people in the years since they've arrived."

She stared at Tarben. This was the prime hunter? He didn't look old enough. At the most, he looked thirty. Not the hunter Anja had said was near a hundred years old. Her friends had told her those who had magic had double the lifespan of the rest of the villagers, but she'd pictured wizened hunters with wrinkled skin and gnarled hands. Somehow, she managed to keep her expression blank.

Another hunter became visible. "About twenty warriors are headed this way. We need to leave. Now."

"Take her to the village," Jorn said. "We should question her."

The same hunter pointed at Jorn. "You haven't been a hunter long enough for your voice to count."

"The voices of all hunters count. From my champions all the way down to those in training," Tarben said.

"Whatever we're going to do, we need to do it now," the hunter who'd warned them said.

As much as Morgane wanted to be taken away from the area of the castle, she didn't want to endanger Anja or Elin. Nor Jorn. Not after he'd saved her. "Either kill me or leave me behind. But don't take me to your village. Brigitte can find me."

Tarben stared at her for a moment, before looking past her. "Everyone scatter. I'll deal with her and meet you at the village."

"Tarben-"

Tarben interrupted Jorn. "You included." Tarben grabbed hold of Morgane's arm and pulled her close. "Remain silent."

She frowned, the light seeming to bend around them. The rest of the hunters vanished, leaving only Jorn and Anja. She stared at them, willing them to leave. For a fraction of time, she managed to make contact with Jorn, sharing with him what she could see.

With a nod, Jorn vanished, along with Anja.

Morgane glanced around. The light Tarben continued to hold was bright enough she could clearly see what was nearby. There were only trees and shrubs. Time stretched out and she wondered if she should ask him what they were doing. Did he plan to stand here all night keeping the two of them invisible? It didn't make sense.

Warriors burst through the trees, pitch torches held aloft. "We're wasting our time. The way those devils disappear they could be right in front of us."

Several warriors agreed with him.

Morgane grinned. He was wrong. They were right behind them.

Warriors spread out, slashing at the air around them with their swords, moving further away, muttering complaints. When the last of their voices could no longer be heard nearby, Tarben released her.

The light went back to normal and she assumed they were no longer invisible. Remaining silent, she met Tarben's gaze. He continued to keep the ball of light in his hand. How powerful was his magic? When he didn't speak, only continued to stare back at her, she kept her expression blank. If it wasn't for the bracelet, she might have considered probing his mind to see what he thought. Even though she doubted she'd be able to get past whatever barrier hunters erected with the help of their magic.

Sensing Jorn behind her, Morgane barely managed to resist the urge to turn and see what he was doing. He must be very close if she could sense him. Then he was beside her and she could tell by the lack of movement out of the corner of her vision that he was invisible. What was he planning? Or either of them planning? She didn't know enough about humans to have any idea how they thought. Gilda didn't count. She'd served dragons long enough she'd probably forgotten centuries ago what it felt like to be human.

"Do you think I cannot sense your signature, Jorn?" Tarben asked. "I know the signature of everyone in the village."

Jorn appeared at Morgane's side. "Everyone has returned to the village."

Tarben looked him up and down. "Obviously not everyone."

"I need to know what you plan to do with her." Jorn nodded in Morgane's direction.

"How is it any concern of yours?" Tarben asked.

Jorn didn't answer immediately. "I owe her a debt. As does Anja and four of our people."

"It hasn't been established yet whether or not she truly did rescue them." Tarben glanced at Morgane before returning his attention to Jorn. "And your debt? What is it?"

"A life debt. Two of them."

Tarben stared at Jorn for an exceptionally long time.

Morgane was surprised he managed to remain still under the scrutiny.

"Do you swear this?" Tarben asked. "On your life, on your magic, on the life of those you hold close."

"I was hunting her this afternoon. She could have easily led me into a trap. Instead, she led me away from it and shapeshifted into a dragon so she could carry me from the warriors who would have attacked me."

"And the second debt?" Tarben asked.

"I told her where to set me down. It wasn't as safe as I assessed it to be. Instead of leaving me to face death alone, she fought at my side until she could once again fly me to safety."

She wanted to protest that it hadn't exactly been like that. It made her sound more accomplished than she'd been.

"Why would she do this for a human? We all know how little they think of us and how they see us as game to be hunted for entertainment," Tarben said.

She wanted to protest that they weren't like that.

Wanted to tell him the humans taken today had been to punish her. Look at how many humans worked at the castle. But she had a feeling Gilda had been sheltering her far more than she should have.

"Why don't you ask her?" Jorn asked.

Tarben met her gaze. "Well?"

She remained silent, not willing to exchange her friends for her life.

"Tell him the truth," Jorn said softly. "He knows it anyway."

Startled, she looked at Jorn. Again she tried to reach his mind. She wanted to curse the bracelet. She didn't have as strong a connection with him as she did with Anja so she was unable to push past the limitations the bracelet put on her.

Jorn stepped close, gripping her shoulder. "The entire truth."

She made contact with his mind the moment his hand pressed against her shoulder. *"Elin? Anja? It won't get them in trouble?"*

"No more than they are already in. He knows. Not everyone in the village does, but he's one of the few who do and is part of the debate as to what will happen to them. Claim leniency for them in exchange for the other four lives you saved tonight."

"Do you have nothing to say for yourself?" Tarben demanded. "I've wasted enough of this night."

"I saved him for Elin. And for Anja, but mostly for Elin. How could I let the brother and cousin of my friends die?" She kept her gaze on Tarben. When Jorn's grip momentarily tightened on her shoulder she didn't dare look at him. "I learned recently that they're in trouble for the time they've spent with me. I ask you to show them leniency in exchange for the four lives I saved tonight."

Tarben glanced at Jorn. "Let her speak for herself."

She raised her chin, looking directly into Tarben's dark eyes. "I do speak for myself. All I want to do is protect Elin and Anja. The family of my heart."

Tarben again glanced at Jorn.

"You don't need to look at Jorn. The words are mine."

Tarben studied her for a moment. "Does that mean you'd be willing to fight against the family of your blood to protect the family of your heart?"

Gilda was right. There was no way she could take the life of Brigitte. No matter what she'd done. She didn't have the ruthless edge most dragons had. But that didn't mean she wasn't a dragon. Neither did it mean she'd let Brigitte go after Elin and Anja. Or Jorn. "I might have something to help you against the dragons if you promise never to use it against me. Or to share it amongst the entire village. Only the two of you." That was providing no one had found the body of her brother. She doubted the warriors she'd killed earlier remained out the front of the castle. Not that she was certain she could move the body of a dragon while she wore the bracelet.

"How would this object help us against the dragons?" Tarben asked.

"If you can find a way for them to consume it, then it will weaken them. It can be hidden in food or drink." She started to tell them it could be smeared across an open wound, but she'd given them more than enough details.

An image of her brother came to mind and she pushed it aside. She really didn't want to cut apart her brother's body so she could grind his bones into a powder to use against other dragons. But if she couldn't find a dragon she could use instead, she'd somehow force herself to use her brother if they set her free and protected her friends. She wasn't about to let someone else she cared about die without trying to save them.

"And what is this miracle ingredient?" Tarben asked.

Morgane remained silent. Telling them would be crazy.

"You expect us to trust you?" Tarben closed the distance between them, looking directly into her eyes. "You hide things from us."

"Do you not hide things from me?" She wanted to push him away from her, but doubted that would help. When Jorn's grip momentarily tightened on her shoulder, she wondered if he'd sensed her thoughts.

"I'll go with her and make sure she gets the ingredient for us," Jorn said.

"I have to wonder at your loyalty." Tarben's gaze focused for a moment on Jorn's hand that remained on her shoulder. "What do you hide, Jorn?"

"I've always been loyal to the village. As has my family."

Morgane managed not to wince when Jorn's fingers dug into the flesh of her shoulder. Would Tarben hear them if she spoke in Jorn's mind? Normally she wouldn't have thought twice about doing so, but she worried the bracelet would reduce her skill at preventing her thoughts from being broadcast when she shared them with someone. Especially with someone as powerful as Tarben in front of her.

"How well do you think of your sister, I wonder?" Tarben asked.

"She's the family of my blood and the family of my heart," Jorn said.

Morgane fought against the pain his words caused to arrow through her. She'd once had a brother who'd felt that way. Keeping her breathing even, she focused on Jorn's hand that once more tightened on her shoulder. "If I give you this ingredient, you will allow me to go my own way and not punish Elin or Anja for the time they've spent with me over the years."

"You wouldn't be allowed to remain in our forests," Tarben said. "And you would need to give us enough of the ingredient that we can use it on every dragon in the castle."

She'd somehow find a way to warn Gilda that she needed to escape. "I'll give you enough to weaken sixty dragons. More than you need. But I will need time to get the ingredient."

"A few days," Tarben offered.

She shook her head. The bones needed to be dried before they could be ground to a powder. She could speed up the process by shaving pieces off with her dagger and drying them by a fire, but there was always the possibility that things might go wrong.

"The turn of the moon." That should give her plenty of time to spare.

"Are you hoping we'll be dead before you can return?" Tarben demanded.

"Get rid of the traitor in your village and you might have less to worry about." When Jorn's grip tightened unnecessarily hard on her shoulder she wanted to tell him to let go of her. She hadn't said anything wrong. Only spoken the truth Anja had shared with her.

"There are no traitors in our village." Tarben's tone matched the disdainful look he gave her. "If this is a ruse to escape, Elin and Anja will pay with their lives."

Chapter Eight

Fear ricocheted through Morgane. "Kill me now. How can I predict the future? What if I'm detained or killed in the process of getting the ingredient for you?" It was a very real possibility since she'd have to go near the castle to fetch her brother's body. "Well? You heard me. Kill me."

Tarben studied her again, frowning. He inclined his head. "I accept. The two of you have till the turn of the moon for one of you to return with the ingredient."

Before Morgane could protest, Tarben vanished, taking the light with him. She stepped forward, hand outstretched as she tried to find him. The small amount of light filtering through the trees did little to help. Normally she could see a lot better than this in the night. The bracelet was causing her a lot of problems. She glanced around the area even though she knew she wouldn't be able to spot Tarben while he was invisible. Or see any depressions in the ground that he might make with the limited amount of light available. "I didn't agree."

"You have no choice. The deal's been made." Jorn remained at her side.

Morgane spun to face him. "This is your sister's life you're gambling with."

"Then I suggest we get started. Where do we need to go to get the ingredient?"

She wanted to protest. Instead, she placed a hand against his chest, reaching for his mind, initially unable to find it. *"Is he still around here?"*

"I don't know. We should move instead of standing here like two lovestruck people."

"It's more than finding an ingredient. I have to go far enough from the castle that Brigitte can't find me while I prepare it."

"We'll find a clearing so you can turn into a dragon."

She couldn't immediately answer him. Didn't want to tell anyone about her problems. *"I can't."*

"You're a dragon. What do you mean you can't?"

She held out her hand with the bracelet. The dull silver metal caught a stray shaft of light, momentarily gleaming. *"This. One of your hunters helped Brigitte to create it."*

He wrapped a hand around the metal. *"Not one of our hunters. Traitors are the enemy."*

The metal warmed against her skin. She pulled away from him. "What are you doing?" She spoke the words aloud, not wanting to be close enough to speak in his mind. What if he made the problem worse? She didn't want to be stuck with the bracelet.

"Where do we need to go first?" Jorn asked.

"We could be gone for days. Do you need to gather anything to take with you?" She gestured in the direction of the village.

"I have my waterskin, bow, some arrows, a dagger and flint and steel. It's everything I need." He paused a moment. "Where do we need to go?"

She struggled for calm, but the thought of what she had to do, made it impossible to achieve. Gwynham would have done anything for her. Like she would have done the same for him. But this felt wrong. "I need to return to the castle."

"Inside it?"

"I hope not." She faced the direction they needed to take. "You can wait here if you want."

"Until we have the ingredient, I'll be closer than a lover." His arm brushed against hers as if to emphasise his point.

A shudder ran through her at the threat in his

voice. Not because of what she feared he might do, but at the thought that eventually they'd have the dragon bone and she'd be alone. Completely alone. She'd never been alone before in her entire life. Even during sleep Gilda had been close enough she could hear her soft sounds and her brother had only been a thought away, their dreams often entangled as they slept.

"Well? I was up early this morning. I'm hoping to get some rest before morning comes again," Jorn said.

Drawing in a slow, deep breath, Morgane headed through the forest towards the castle. They were closer than she'd realised. The bracelet must be messing with her sense of location too. How did humans function? She stopped at the edge of the treeline, peering out at the ground in front of the castle. They hadn't collected the bodies of the dragons? Surely they should have collected them by now.

"What are you waiting for?"

"Something is wrong."

"What?"

"I don't know. Normally I'd try and contact Gilda and if she was close enough she could tell me."

"Then contact her."

Morgane held up the bracelet in answer. "I can't

even sense where you are unless you're close. I should be able to sense you from half a day's walk away."

"From my blood you stole."

She inclined her head.

"Would more blood help?"

"You'd give me more blood?"

Jorn grinned. "I'm interested in learning the limitations of that bracelet. Maybe we can create ways of neutralising you dragons."

She drew her dagger, not caring that his reasons didn't match hers. She wanted to know the limitations too. Needed to know what she was capable of. Since hunters had helped create it, maybe the blood of a hunter might help in some way. "I'm willing to try."

He hesitated before holding out his hand. "Maybe I should be the one to wield the blade." He held out his other hand.

She gave him the dagger and watched as he made a nick in his arm, the blood welling up dark against his skin. The sharp metallic smell filled the air around them and she lowered her head, pressing her mouth to the wound.

"Do you notice any difference?" He said the words in her mind.

She kept drinking, the blood a trickle, the coppery

taste filling her mouth. It reminded her that she'd barely eaten and her stomach rumbled softly.

Jorn tried to pull his arm from her grip. "I am not on the menu."

She tightened her hold on him, lapping at the blood that continued to trickle from the cut. *"How can you expect to know if there's a difference if you want to end the experiment partway through the process?"* She spoke into his mind, not daring to stop in case he managed to break free.

"Is it your plan to weaken me?" Jorn spoke the words aloud. "Why save my life twice only to kill me this way?"

"Do all hunters whine and complain this much?" Not sure she'd consumed enough blood for it to make a difference, yet not daring to take any more, she lifted her head, continuing to hold onto his arm.

He wrapped his other hand around her bracelet. "Let go of me."

She felt the metal warm against her skin. Before she could protest, her vision brightened and she could see the world more clearly. "What are you doing?" Whatever it was, it seemed to be having a positive effect. She felt stronger, sounds were sharper and the smells around her were clearer.

"What are you planning, Morgane?"

She looked sharply in the direction of the castle at hearing Brigitte's voice in her head. When Jorn let go of her, the metal cooled and her senses lessened. She also no longer felt the presence of Brigitte. She grabbed hold of Jorn's hand, placing it back on the bracelet. "Whatever you did, do it again."

"You should have collapsed on the ground. Whatever that metal is, it does something strange to magic."

"You tried to hurt me?"

"I thought you planned to drink more of my blood."

She stepped close to him, toe to toe. "If Elin didn't love you…" She left the threat hanging.

"What could you do while wearing that?" Jorn nodded towards the bracelet.

Still feeling the effects of the magic he'd poured into her, she had him pinned to the ground in the blink of an eye, his hands above his head and held by one of her hands while she pressed a dagger at his throat. "I am not helpless."

"Neither am I."

She felt the heat of his magic against her hands, her body absorbing the energy generated. A grin formed and she kept him pinned to the ground as she mentally searched for Gilda. It didn't take long to locate the woman. She was in the small room off her bedroom that Gilda slept in. *"What is happening?"* She could feel Brigitte trying to join the conversation. The magic Jorn continued to use against her fuelled her own ability.

"Morgane? How is this possible? Did you learn the word Brigitte used to seal the bracelet?"

"That isn't important right now. What is happening at the castle?"

"Brigitte learned you've taken Gwynham's body. Everyone is searching for it. They believe it's on the grounds since no one saw you with him when you attacked them out the front."

"Is that why the dead are still in front of the castle?" Morgane ignored Jorn's demands to let him go, pressing him harder against the ground as he struggled against her grip.

"There were some complaints about leaving their fellow warriors to lie on the ground instead of bringing them inside. They will find where you've hidden Gwynham so they can deal with the dead."

"Thank you, Gilda." Morgane hesitated. *"You must find somewhere else to live. It's not safe for you there."*

"I have nowhere else to go. I've spent my entire life in service to your family."

"Gilda, you can't–"

Gilda interrupted her. *"Your mother is here. She knows you're talking to me. She wants me to give you a message. Warriors are coming to collect you. They know where you are. And you can't run faster than they can fly."* Gilda paused a moment. *"Flee, Morgane. Live. One of you must live. Don't let me fail this too."*

Morgane broke the connection, sheathing her dagger when a line of blood formed beneath it on Jorn's throat. "Warriors are coming for us. They know where we are." Before letting him up, she lowered her head and licked the blood from his throat. Grinning, she rose to her feet, retreating from his reach. "No point wasting it." Not that it seemed to help. No, it was his magic she needed. Her gaze was drawn to his hands before returning to his face. Her grin widened at the anger she saw in his eyes. She doubted he'd ever think her helpless again.

"How do you know they're coming?"

Breaking into a run towards one of the dead warriors, at the front of the castle, she debated sharing the information with him. She glanced at him when he came alongside her. "Your magic is like kindling to a dying fire."

"I'm surprised you told me."

She glanced at Jorn. "You shouldn't be. Until your

sister's life is safe again, I'll do whatever it takes to ensure I'm not the reason she's harmed. What are you willing to do?"

"Work with a dragon."

His dry tone had her lips curving slightly. The smile never had a chance to form. The sky filled with dragons. "We need one of those warriors." She gestured towards the dead dragon they ran towards. "I don't suppose you can use your magic to take him with you while I lead them away."

"Where will we meet up?"

"Near running water."

Reaching the dragon, Jorn placed a hand on him and they both vanished. "I'll meet you at the fork of the river."

Before she could protest how far away that was, a hand momentarily rested on her arm and images filled her mind. Sticks and stones set out in almost natural looking patterns. "What do they mean?"

"They give directions." He removed his hand from her arm, but not before giving her more information about each of the images.

Dragons swooped down towards her and she raced in close to the castle, using it as a shield. They banked at the last moment as she raced along the stone wall, heading around the corner. Her sense of Jorn faded and she didn't know if it was because they were moving away from each other, because the magic was wearing off or a mixture of both.

A dragon landed in front of Morgane, becoming human. He drew a sword from the scabbard at his side. "She doesn't care what condition you're in as long as you can talk when I throw you at her feet."

Chapter Nine

Mentally cursing the bracelet, Morgane reached for her bow. He was faster than her, his blade causing her to stumble backwards, bow untouched. She could have done with a hunter's ability of being able to bend the light around their body to hide them from sight.

The warrior attacked again. She dodged, a rush of air from the blade brushing her face. He renewed his efforts, driving her towards the corner she'd come around. He stopped mid attack, looking up at a dragon flying overhead before running away from the wall of the castle to turn and face it.

Morgane caught the scent of smoke and as much as she was tempted to join the warrior who stared up at the castle, she took the opportunity to run towards the back of the castle and the pond. Although how she'd managed to fetch her brother's body unnoticed, she had no idea. Panicked shouts reached her as she turned the corner and left the safety of the castle walls behind, sprinting towards the pond. A glance over her shoulder had her stumbling. Flames were visible through several windows of the castle, the smell of smoke growing stronger, plumes of smoke pouring out of the windows.

Focusing on the ground ahead, she continued towards the pond. The only person who'd help was Gilda. She dreaded to think what Brigitte would do to her for this. A glance over her shoulder showed no one pursued her. All the dragons were flying back to the castle.

She tried to reach Gilda. It was impossible. The effects from the magic had mostly worn off. She needed to get Gwynham's body and get out of here. Reaching the pond, she plunged into the water, the chill seeping into her body, the night having grown cooler. Even her ability to keep her temperature up was affected by the bracelet.

Another glance over her shoulder showed that still no one pursued. The flames continued to dance in the windows and smoke poured from the openings. How many fires had Gilda set? When the water reached her chest, she sank beneath the surface, swimming towards the spot where she thought her brother's body lay. She tried to sense where it was, but failed. Swimming further out, her lungs bursting, she strained to see in the depths of the pond. It was hard enough to see during the day, near impossible right now.

Shooting towards the surface, she gulped air before again swimming to the bottom of the pond. Her hands brushed across the silt and rocks lining the bottom of the pond. But she couldn't find the cloth wrapped body of her brother. Again she was forced to surface for more air. This time she looked around, trying to use landmarks to better locate where he was. It didn't help. She was sure this was where he'd sunk. A glance towards the castle showed the fire had lessened and the smoke had reduced. She didn't have long. If she didn't find him soon, she'd have to leave him behind. Pain and anger swirled through her. It was the last thing she wanted to do.

Taking a deep breath, she swam to the bottom again. She strained her senses, trying to find where he was. There was a slight tug to her left. Swimming in that direction, she closed her eyes, focusing completely on her senses. Her fingers collided with a different object, neither rock nor silt. Opening her eyes didn't help. She ran her hands over the object. Her senses flared to life. It was her brother. Wrapping her arms around his body, she struggled to take him to the surface. Her lungs burned from lack of air and she felt dizzy. Yet she didn't dare let him go. How could Brigitte have done this to her? She was meant to be her daughter, not the enemy.

A memory came to mind, Brigitte towering over her and Gwynham, anger glinting in her eyes, her voice low and harsh. 'Everyone is the enemy. Allies are temporary. It is only humans who don't know this. You two are dragons. There will come a day when one of you will turn on the other. It's inevitable.' She'd strode from the room and Gwynham had taken her hand. Neither of them had spoken. Not aloud and not in their minds. They hadn't needed to. They'd known Brigitte was wrong. It wasn't inevitable.

Breaking the surface, Morgane gulped lungfuls of air. She scanned her surroundings. In the sky above the castle, dragons circled. Were they starting the search again? She didn't know, but wasn't about to wait around to find out. Holding her brother's body with one arm, she struck out for the bank, struggling to keep him from sinking again.

Reaching the edge of the pond, she spared a glance for the castle before staggering out of the water, dragging Gwynham with her. The dragons were still overhead. Hopefully, there was time before they hunted her down again. Lifting her brother's body into her arms, she strode towards the forest, exhaustion dragging at her like the water soaked body of her brother dragged at her arms.

How did humans survive with their limited abilities and weak bodies? Even stronger than them, with her lessened abilities, she felt pathetic and useless. Anger curled through her. She wasn't about to let Brigitte get away with all she'd done. It wasn't her fault and nor had it been Gwynham's that Brigitte's father had stranded her in this world for falling in love with the wrong dragon. And nor was it any of their faults that he'd somehow figured out a way to close this world off from all other worlds, making it impossible for Dorran to enter the void.

At first, Brigitte had railed against Dorran, according to the stories Gilda had told, accusing him of lying. Eventually, he'd convinced her that his years of service were done and no one was coming to take over from him and he couldn't leave. None of them had been able to figure out what Brigitte's father had done to shut them off from the rest of the worlds and make it impossible for them to access the void. Not even the hunters Dorran had captured and threatened had been able to figure anything out.

Morgane glanced over her shoulder as she staggered past the treeline, wishing she could lower her brother to the ground and rest. But the dragons were coming this way. There would be no rest. Remaining amongst the trees, she turned in the direction of the river fork, placing one foot in front of the other as she ignored the ache in her arms.

Time seemed to drag out, the muscles in her shoulders aching as much as the ones in her arms and eventually the ones down her back and legs. All the while she forced herself forward, ignoring the ache and moving as fast as was humanly possible. Which was a lot slower than was possible for a dragon. And probably slower than a hunter.

Several times she had to force herself into a run to avoid the searching warriors and a couple of times she hid up a tree, having placed her brother's body under a dense shrub. As much as she'd appreciated the rests, the effort to remain still and not make a sound had been excruciating. She didn't want to be human. Didn't want to give up the power of being a dragon and the ability to fly through the skies. Eventually, she lost her pursuers and managed to travel beyond the range that Brigitte could track her. Which was a lot less than the range she was normally capable of. It had annoyed Brigitte each time she'd done something better than her so she'd always tried avoiding letting her know when she excelled at anything. It had been safer that way. Her gaze was drawn to Gwynham. For both of them. She fought against the pain that threatened to swamp her. Safer until Brigitte had wanted their hearts.

She had no idea how close it was to sunrise, but knew it had to be well after the middle of the night when she stumbled out of the forest and onto the banks of the river. She couldn't see Jorn anywhere. Or the dragon he was meant to bring with him. She lowered her brother's body to the ground. A thought struck her. What if the bone of a dragon warrior didn't work in this world? Like only the heart of a Gold worked to stop the aging process here. What if they needed to be the bones of a Gold? Sinking to the ground beside her brother she wrapped her arms around herself. She didn't know if she could do it. After everything that had happened, all she wanted to do was mourn Gwynham then make sure Brigitte and Dorran couldn't do this to another. Either her or any children they had. The best way to do that was to kill Dorran and then Brigitte would have no Gold to have children with. Brigitte would have to be desperate to turn to one of those she called common warriors.

Morgane's body trembled with exhaustion and she leaned against the trunk of the tree that was behind her, closing her eyes. If only her father had come for them like Brigitte had told her he'd promised to do. The man Brigitte now cursed for not keeping his promise. Although to be fair, from the stories she'd been told, he hadn't set a time of when he'd arrive. Only told Brigitte he'd come for her as soon as he could. That he'd find a way of helping her escape this world. Gilda was the one who'd told them their father hadn't been a Gold. He'd been a common warrior. Which surprised Morgane considering Brigitte's current hatred of them. But maybe that was part of the reason for her hatred.

She sank further against the tree. Her thoughts drifted and her breathing slowed, the sound of the river soothing. She had no idea when she drifted off, but a hand on her shoulder jarred her awake, the grey of early morning filling the sky. Heart racing she looked around to find no one. It took her a moment to realise she could sense Jorn. "Where were you?"

He appeared beside her, his hand remaining on her shoulder. "Any hunter could have slit your throat." Lifting his hand from her shoulder, he tugged on a lock of hair that had escaped from beneath her dragon-leather scarf. "None of our people have hair this fair unless they're very old. And you don't look in the least bit aged."

Tugging the strands from his fingers, she glanced at the cloth wrapped body of her brother. "Where is the warrior you took with you?"

"In a cave not far from here. I left signs for you to follow." He gestured towards a cluster of sticks and stones by the river. "Didn't you see them?"

"No." She wasn't a hunter, how could he have expected her to notice them amongst everything else? She was a dragon. Her gaze was drawn to the bracelet. And one day soon she'd be able to take her dragon form again.

"I'll break the signs apart when I show you to the cave. We don't need anyone else following us." He nodded towards the body. "And the human?"

"Dragon."

"They're dead."

She inclined her head, staggering to her feet, barely managing not to moan at the various aches and pains. Who would want to be human? Their bodies were so limiting and frail.

Jorn stepped in front of her when she moved towards the body. "How can they be a dragon? You always shift to your dragon form when you die."

It was the last thing she wanted to talk about. "My

brother wears one of these bracelets too." She glanced at the object on her wrist before stepping around Jorn and reaching for Gwynham.

Jorn tugged her back. "This is your brother?" He gestured towards the body.

She struggled to keep her feelings neutral and her expression blank. "Yes." She started to congratulate herself on how expressionless she'd managed to make the word.

"That is why I can feel so much pain inside you."

"You can-" She broke off, shaking her head. "No. You can't."

He lifted her arm he still held, his hand warm through the dragon-leather of her shirt. "When I come in contact with you. Pain so extreme it feels like someone has driven a sword through you repeatedly." He frowned. "And you're cold and damp. When I first met you, your temperature felt like you might have a fever. Or you would if you were human."

She dragged her arm from his grip. She'd been certain she'd contained the pain a lot better than that. "Where is the cave?" Again she tried to move past Jorn to pick up Gwynham.

Jorn stepped in front of her, gathering Gwynham before she could. "This way." He walked past the sticks and stones, kicking them apart before heading into the forest.

She followed him, feeling like she should protest. Not knowing if she could carry her brother another step, she remained silent.

Several times Jorn stopped to kick apart groupings of sticks and stones, eventually leading them into a cave, a fire burning at the entrance. "Help yourself to the rabbit I left warming at the edge of the coals." He set Gwynham down beside the bulky body of the dragon that took up a large section of the cave.

She crouched by the fire, the warmth sinking into her as she reached for the meat. "Should you have a fire burning? Won't someone notice?"

Jorn shrugged as he joined her by the fire. "I can vanish."

She met his gaze. "I can't." She glanced over her shoulder. "Nor can they." She tried not to think about the many things her brother would never be able to do.

"Why do we need the dead warrior?"

Chapter Ten

Morgane stared into the flames, not wanting to tell Jorn all her secrets. What would he do with them? Would he one day use them against her?

"Morgane?" He rested his hand on her arm. "I understand not wanting to leave your brother's body behind, but why do we need the other one?"

Setting aside the rest of the meat, she met his gaze. "Would you keep my secrets from your people?"

He didn't answer her immediately, removing his hand from her arm before he spoke. "No." The word was flat and inflexible.

"That's what I thought." She looked away from him, her gaze drawn to the light increasing outside the cave. "Do hunters use this cave often?"

"Rarely. It's too close to the savages."

"So we should be safe here?" She kept her gaze on the scenery.

"Outside a village nowhere is truly safe. Inside a village, it is only those by your side keeping you safe."

Her gaze was drawn to him, unable to resist studying him. "You truly believe that."

"That it isn't safe outside a village?"

"No. That those by your side would protect you."

He nodded, a frown forming. "Don't you believe the same? That those you stand with will stand with you."

"No." She glanced at the cloth wrapped body. She'd known that once. But she kept those words to herself as she struggled to contain the pain.

He closed the distance between them, clasping her hand in his. "This is why my sister was drawn to you. She could never resist an injured animal. Even one that should be hunted for food."

She wrenched her hand from his. "I am not an injured animal."

"How can you say that with the constant pain I feel rolling off you? I didn't even need to be in contact that time."

"I lost my brother." The words were torn from her. "Would you be able to set it aside if you lost your sister?" And yet she shouldn't be able to feel such pain. The anger should drown it out. It didn't. Was

Brigitte right? No, she was a dragon. "Would you easily forget that you had a sister?"

"No. I'd want to make them pay for every bit of pain I felt." His voice was hard, his gaze meeting hers. "Why haven't you done that?"

"Would you be able to kill your mother?"

He opened his mouth, but only a soft sound of surprise escaped.

She laughed, a bitter noise that echoed in the cave. "I guess not." She returned to looking at the scenery, unable to discuss it further.

"Your mother killed one of her children."

She didn't bother answering. His tone had been one of disbelief. What could she say that would make him believe? What did she want to say? Images from her childhood flashed through her mind. The many things done to make her and Gwynham turn against each other. To learn that amongst dragons the only one you could trust was yourself. She flinched when Jorn rested a hand on her shoulder.

"Why do you care for Elin and Anja? You're a dragon, aren't you? A full dragon."

"Because they never treated me like a dragon." At first it had intrigued her and eventually it had echoed what her and Gwynham had. When Jorn didn't comment, she turned her head to look at him.

Would he think he could befriend all dragons? That would get him killed. "I might be a full dragon, but I'm only half Gold. Dorran might say that you're either Gold or not, but it makes a difference when only one of your parents is Gold. The bloodline is no longer pure. Brigitte is the only pure Gold left in this world. Your people killed the three pure Golds that arrived here with her. She'll never forgive them for that. And her warriors would never go against her."

"They captured my people and forced them to build their castle. When they refused, they slaughtered their family in front of them. My people will never forgive dragons for that." He held her gaze a moment. "No matter what you do to help us, it won't undo all the slaughter that occurred before you were born."

She tilted her head slightly as she played his words over in her mind, trying to figure out what his tone meant. "A warning?"

He shrugged, removing his hand from her shoulder. "Take it how you will." He gestured towards the dead warrior. "What will you do with him? Eventually, he'll begin to rot." He glanced at the cloth wrapped body, not saying anything.

She didn't need him to point out the same would

happen to Gwynham. "Can you gather wood? I need to make a funeral pyre."

"Near the cave?"

"Somewhere nearby that won't give away our location."

"What will you be doing while I collect wood?"

Her gaze was drawn to the two bodies. One large and draconic, the other slim and human. Her brother didn't deserve to die a human. He was a dragon. "You really don't want to know." She rose to her feet. "Can you help me drag the warrior outside?"

"I've got him." Jorn placed his hands against the scales and the dragon rose above the ground, moving ahead of Jorn as he guided him outside the cave, lowering him to the ground before he stopped pressing his hands against him.

Before following him outside, she took off her rucksack and set it and the gear from it out by the fire to dry. The food was no good. She tossed it into the fire rather than leave it lying around to draw in creatures. The dragons would be tempting enough.

Jorn faced Morgane when she joined him. "I'll be back shortly with wood for the campfire first."

She wanted to protest. Wanted to get the process over and done with. While he was gone, she carved into the dragon's skin, removing the paw so she could get at the smaller bones. Ones it'd be easier to crush. By the time Jorn returned, she had several pieces of bone scraped off and set aside.

Jorn glanced at the dragon, his gaze resting on the bloody stump before building up the fire and leaving again.

She stared at the trees he'd headed through, having remained visible. He hadn't said a word. She'd expected him to say something. Ask a question at least. She didn't know if she should be worried about that. Elin and Anja had always been curious, but did that mean all humans were?

Picking up the bone shavings, she glanced around the area one more time before she popped them in her mouth, bracing herself for the inevitable weakness she'd been told they'd bring. Nothing happened. Had she consumed enough? She'd been told a few scrapings was all it'd take. Had that been a false threat Brigitte had used to drive them apart? No, surely not. Gilda had warned them they must never eat dragon bone. Anything else they could eat. Just not the bone. She scraped off some more, eating it like the last pieces. Still nothing happened. Her gaze was drawn to the cave opening, the area past the fire was filled with shadows, the body of her brother hidden from view.

She remained where she was, unable to bring herself to enter the cave and bring Gwynham's body outside. She wanted to curl up by the fire and lose herself to sleep. One of Brigitte's taunts came to mind. 'Not much of a dragon. Must be the taint of your father's blood. Never trust a charming smile. Look what I've ended up with in return. Two useless children that might as well be human.' She closed her eyes as she tried to push away the memories. The last time Brigitte had snarled the words, Gwynham had waited until she'd stalked off before slipping an arm around her shoulders, tilting his head close to hers and grinning at her. She hadn't needed any words from her brother. Had known from his expression and the look in his blue eyes that he'd been mocking Brigitte.

Pain arrowed through her, but none of the expected weakness arrived. She didn't want to carve into her brother's body. She wanted to let the flames of a funeral pyre consume him so no one could use any of him for their own gain. Then she wanted to hunt down his heart and do the same to it.

Forcing herself to her feet, she walked unsteadily to the cave, pausing at the entrance. Exhaustion tugged at her. She wanted to sleep. Wanted to turn into a dragon and fly far from here. Wanted her dragon abilities back. Especially the one of fast healing.

It took all her willpower to gather up her brother's body and take him outside, lying him on the ground next to the warrior. Using her dagger, she slit open the cloth, trying not to look too closely at Gwynham. If she didn't think about it, then surely she'd manage to do what had to be done. Elin and Anja. She had to focus on them. Focus on a way to keep them safe. Her attention was caught by his bracelet and anger raced through her. Even in death he was shackled by it. Gritting her teeth, she cut into the flesh of his wrist, continuing through until flesh, muscle and bone were no longer held together and the hand became a dragon paw. Dropping it to the ground, she tugged on the bracelet, knocked backwards when the human form became dragon.

Tears came to her eyes at the sight of the gold flecked silver dragon. She wanted to throw herself at him and beg him to wake. But there was no heart to beat. Closing her eyes, she took deep breaths, focusing on her surroundings to take her mind off what had to be done. The sounds of the forest creatures came to her, muted and muffled, many of them blending together. Normally she'd be able to focus on individual sounds, pinpointing exactly where they came from. Another wave of anger rushed through her, pushing away the sorrow. Nothing could drown the pain.

Opening her eyes, she picked up the silver dragon paw, cutting through flesh to the bone beneath, scraping fragments away. Taking a deep breath, she ate them. Energy rushed through her instead of the sickness she'd expected, the sounds around her sharpening. Exhaustion faded, along with aches and physical pain. Had it all been a lie? Had it been a way to hide the unimaginable power in the bones of a gold? Surely not. Gilda had never lied to them. She'd refused to tell them things, but had never outright lied. Unless of course someone had lied to her.

"What are you doing?"

She'd been so busy focusing on the tiny sounds out in the forest that she hadn't taken note of what was happening close by. Now she was taking note, she sensed Jorn on the other side of the warrior, invisible. "Show yourself."

Visible, Jorn stepped around the warrior, avoiding the blood pooling on the ground. "What are you doing?"

"We need a live dragon. One of the warriors."

"Why?" He gestured to the dead warrior. "What's wrong with him?"

"He's dead." She wanted to ask him how long he'd

been watching. Had he seen her struggling to cut off her brother's hand?

"I thought you wanted one that was dead."

"Now I need one that's alive."

He crossed the space separating them. "What are you planning? You can't expect me to go running around doing your bidding when I have no reason to trust you."

"What about owing me for saving your life?"

"So now I should let you throw it away?"

A sound had her spinning, grabbing an arrow out of mid-air. She started to take a step forward, stopped from doing so by Jorn who grabbed hold of her arm. Before she could protest, the light bent around them and he tugged her towards the cave. *"We have to track them down, not get trapped in the cave."* She thought the words to him, not wanting to let the hunter know where they were.

"How are we meant to see them while they remain invisible?"

She grabbed his hand, halting his movements, focusing on the sounds around them. Turning her head as she searched, she spotted the depression in the ground. *"I know where the hunter is."*

"How?"

"Look at the ground over there." She used the arrow to point.

"I see no difference."

She looked from the ground to Jorn and back again. Was dragon eyesight really that much better than that of a hunter? She'd thought a hunter's was better than a human's. *"Can't you see the depressions in the ground? Look, he's walking towards us."*

"Can you really see him moving towards us?"

"Yes. Slowly and carefully. You can count to three between each time he moves."

"He's not changing the pattern every now and then?"

She counted out several more steps. *"No."*

"It isn't anyone from our village. That's drummed into us from the start."

"Three steps and he'll be upon us."

"We'll grab him. Being invisible doesn't stop someone from catching you."

She tucked the arrow down the side of her boot before checking her quiver cover was still in place. *"How do we do this? Shall I grab him? Will you be able to see him then?"*

"I'll keep hold of you. Wrap your arms around him so it's impossible for him to bend the light between you. As long as I keep hold of you he'll either have to stop bending

the light around himself or bend it around the three of us. I doubt he'll have the skill to change the number of people he hides so easily." He wrapped an arm around her waist.

Chapter Eleven

Once Jorn was holding on tight, Morgane lunged forward, wrapping her arms around a body that instantly became visible. "You." It was the hunter who'd been at yesterday's cave.

He stopped his struggles. "How do you know me?" He looked past Morgane. "I know you. Traitor. What are you doing with a dragon?"

"We really need to dye your hair to make it a more natural colour," Jorn thought to her.

"What do we do with him?" she thought to Jorn, keeping hold of the hunter.

"Why did you attack?" Jorn asked the hunter.

"She's a dragon. Must be with hair that colour." The hunter's gaze was drawn to the strands escaping around the edges of the dragon-leather scarf.

She cut off Jorn's thoughts to her, pointing out he'd been right. "I suppose you'll object to killing him."

She tightened her grip on the hunter when her words caused him to begin struggling again. Grabbing his arms, when he tried to attack, she pinned them to his sides. The bow was knocked from his grip.

"You will not kill one of my people for no reason," Jorn warned. "No matter what village we're from, we're all one people."

"There is a reason. He'll ruin our plans. It's not like we can tie him up while we hunt down a dragon to experiment on," Morgane said.

"You never mentioned experimenting on the dragon," Jorn said.

"Now you're going to object to harming dragons too?" Morgane demanded.

The hunter stopped struggling again. "You're a dragon."

"I'm well aware of that." Even when she was being told she wasn't a dragon. Although it was kind of nice to have someone say she was. Morgane looked him over. "What are we meant to do with you?"

"Why are you going after dragons?" the hunter asked.

"Long story," Morgane muttered.

"Did you kill those dragons?" The hunter nodded towards the bodies since his arms were trapped.

"One of them." She couldn't bring herself to look at her brother.

"Is that what it takes to kill a dragon? Another dragon?" the hunter asked.

"Our people killed half a dozen dragons when they first arrived in this world," Jorn said.

"Only because you took them by surprise. When was the last time you heard about one of us killing one of them?" the hunter asked. "Look how she plucked my arrow from the air. Is that why you've become her hunting companion? So you can kill dragons. I saw their castle a week ago. I must have counted a dozen dragons in the sky. Why would she betray her people? How do you know she won't turn on you?"

Jorn's arms around Morgane's waist momentarily tightened. "I don't know. I have to believe she'll continue to keep me alive. And we're not hunting companions."

"What are you to her? A slave?" the hunter demanded.

"No." The word burst from Jorn and he let her go, stepping away.

Morgane chuckled, turning her head to look at Jorn. "You wouldn't make a good slave. You'd balk at the first order given." When Jorn continued to stare, her laughter faded. She wanted to demand what he was thinking, but wasn't certain he'd tell her. "We need to decide what to do with this one."

"This one! I have a name. It's–"

She interrupted him. "I'd rather not know in case I have to kill you."

"Cort."

She frowned at him for a moment, initially thinking he meant he was caught. "I told you not to tell me your name."

"If it'll make it harder for you to kill me I'm not about to keep silent about it."

This time it was Jorn who laughed. "Do you really think that will be enough to prevent a dragon from killing you?"

"I don't know. My village is three days from here. There are no dragons in our area. All we have are rumours and myths. I wanted to learn about them for myself. After this, I'm heading north to discover the truth about the creatures of nightmares."

Morgane looked from Cort to Jorn several times, her gaze coming to a rest on Jorn. "Do your people suffer from illnesses of the brain? Should I put him out of his misery before he goes mad?"

"He isn't mad," Jorn said. "He's testing himself."

"How is that a test?" she demanded. "All it will do is get him killed."

"Proving his bravery." Jorn turned his attention to Cort. "Your father must be the prime hunter for you to have chosen something so difficult. How do you plan to prove your actions?"

Cort nodded to the dead dragons. "I was going to take the heads of them after I shot the two of you."

Morgane's eyes narrowed and she tightened her grip on Cort when he struggled to escape again. "What about a live dragon that was weakened enough for you to take home?"

Cort stilled. "You?"

She snorted. "Not in this lifetime."

Cort looked past her to Jorn. "He's not a dragon. I'm pretty sure of it."

"I'm a hunter," Jorn said.

Cort's lips slowly curved into a grin. "You're going to hunt one down?"

"No," Jorn stated.

At the same time, Morgane said, "Yes."

Jorn moved closer to her. "No. We can't risk it."

"I've got an idea." She thought of the arrow in her boot. "The ingredient doesn't need to be consumed, only needs to get into a dragon's bloodstream."

"What ingredient?" Cort asked. "You can let me

go. I'm interested in taking a living dragon home." He looked at Jorn. "Do you promise I can trust the two of you not to attack me? Promise on your magic?"

"I can only speak for myself," Jorn said. "But if you cause no harm to either of us, I have no need to retaliate."

Cort looked to Morgane. "What do dragons promise on?"

"Our word is our law."

"Really?" Cort asked.

"Yes. Which is why we rarely make promises. But I will promise you similar and add in those I am protective of. You harm those I care about and I will rip your heart out." Her gaze hardened. "And I will consume every last bit of it."

Cort swallowed visibly. "I think you mean it."

"You better believe I do." She tried not to think of Gwynham and how she'd never be able to fully avenge him. "Are you satisfied with my offer?"

Cort looked at each of them and then the dead dragons before meeting Morgane's gaze. "Yes. What do I need to do to take a living dragon back to my village?"

Morgane released Cort, taking the arrow from her boot and holding it out to him. "Bring back a deer.

I need some rendered down fat." She looked to Jorn. "Both of you." She started to turn away, drawing her dagger and facing Cort to offer it to him hilt first. "Before you go. I need some of your blood."

Jorn stepped between them, preventing Cort from taking the dagger. "No."

"I will not work with someone who can sneak up on me."

"How long can you use his blood to track him down?"

"A very long time." She smiled. "But have you forgotten the bracelet?"

Jorn held her gaze, speaking directly to her. *"I haven't forgotten. But I notice you don't seem to currently have much of a problem with it. Want to explain that?"*

"Things are working strangely." Her gaze was momentarily drawn to her brother. *"Which is why we need a dragon to experiment on. The ingredient isn't working as it should on me."*

"Are you two going to gaze into each others' eyes all day or are we going to hunt down a deer so we can go after a dragon?" Cort stepped around Jorn to face him. "Is there a reason I shouldn't trust her word? Why should there be a problem with her being able to track me down if I don't hurt her or her loved ones?"

Jorn met Morgane's gaze. "Will there be a problem?"

"If he doesn't cause one, then there won't be one." She held the dagger out to Cort again.

He took it, making a cut at the base of his hand and wiping the dagger against the leg of his trousers before handing it back.

Morgane sheathed the dagger then raised his arm to her lips. She sensed Jorn move close to her before she drank Cort's blood, letting go of his arm once she had the sense of him. "The two of you can go hunting now."

Cort lowered his arm. "That's it?"

"What did you expect? That I'd drink half your blood?" She turned to Jorn, smiling. "Although sometimes a little more is needed."

"*A little?*" Jorn thought the words to her.

Laughing, she turned away, sensing them head into the forest, Cort asking Jorn what was going on. She didn't blame Jorn for not replying. He was probably as confused about what was happening as she was. She needed to figure out how to get rid of the bracelet as soon as possible.

Checking once more where the two of them were, she set to work on scraping bits of bone from the ones she'd removed. When she could no longer sense the two hunters, she had a little bit more of the bone from her brother. A boost in power allowed her to keep track of them as they wandered further afield. It also allowed her to keep her senses sharp so she was aware of everything going on around her. Other than the forest creatures going about their business, no one was in the vicinity.

She set the bone scrapings out to dry, keeping them in two separate piles. The rocks she placed them upon warmed in the sun as the day progressed. By the time Jorn and Cort headed back towards the cave, she had two large piles of bone shavings. They would need to be ground up before they could be used on a warrior.

Not wanting them to know what she'd been up to, she removed the dragon-leather scarf and cut off two sections, putting a nick in one so she could tell the difference between the bone she wrapped in each bit of leather. She tucked them in her belt pouch, her fingers brushing across the lock of hair she'd put in there yesterday. Pain arrowed through her. She pushed it away. She couldn't deal with it right now. There were other things she had to focus on. Like making sure Brigitte and Dorran didn't produce offspring for the sole purpose of eating their hearts.

She was sitting by the campfire, her hair tucked under the dragon-leather scarf, when Jorn and Cort arrived, the deer carried on a branch between them. She started to rise to her feet as they began to skin the deer.

Jorn waved her away. "A third person would get in the way."

Cort glanced at her. "Dragons know how to skin a deer? I thought they ate everything raw. Tearing it apart with their claws and fangs."

Morgane didn't know whether to be amused or offended. "I hate to disappoint you, but we even dress in our best clothes for dinner."

Cort paused in what he was doing, his gaze remaining on her for a moment. "You eat at a table? Off plates and everything."

"On plates of gold and drink wine from goblets," Morgane said.

"Plates of gold." Cort slowly shook his head. "Now that's something I'd like to see."

She studied him for a moment. Did he really mean that? "It would likely be the last thing you ever saw."

Jorn, who continued to work on the deer, glanced at Cort. "Do you expect me to do this on my own?"

Cort returned to helping. "It's all right for you. You've lived around dragons your entire life. I've only ever heard stories and I'm sure most of them have been made up to scare children into behaving."

"I wouldn't count on it," Morgane said bitterly. "The worse the story, the more likely it is to be true." She couldn't resist looking at her brother's body lying in the sun.

"Does that mean we shouldn't trust you?" Cort asked.

She stared at the hunter for a moment, comparing his features to Jorn's. They both had a similar colouring. Where Jorn's shoulders were broad and his jaw square, Cort's was narrower and his shoulders not as wide. "How many years have you lived?"

"Twenty-one. Why?"

She slowly shook her head. "No reason." After talking to him it was hard to believe he was a year older than Jorn. Was that because his village was so far from dragons?

"Is that a warning?" Jorn spoke directly in her mind. *"Are you trying to tell us we're naive for trusting you?"*

She met his gaze, a hardness to his expression she didn't expect. *"Would I save you only to kill you at a later date? Nothing has changed."*

Jorn glanced first at Cort then at the deer before returning his attention to Morgane. *"Things have changed."*

She debated asking him for clarification, but

decided she wasn't certain she wanted to know. She inclined her head.

Cort paused in what he was doing. "I'm missing something, aren't I?" Neither of them answered and he eventually returned to helping Jorn.

Chapter Twelve

Not having anything she could do until Jorn and Cort left, Morgane gathered her cloak that was now mostly dry and headed towards the back of the cave to curl up and sleep. She had no idea how long she slept, but the scent of venison cooking woke her. She sat up to find Jorn nearby. He looked in her direction when she moved. A mental search of the area let her know Cort was outside by the dragons. "What is he doing?"

"Looking for weak points." Jorn nodded towards the fire. "Want something to eat?" He paused a moment. "The fat you asked for is cooling on a piece of bark by the fire."

She started to rise to her feet. "He isn't touching-"

Jorn moved close, taking her hand. "I told him to leave the silver dragon alone."

Relief rushed through her.

"You feel emotions like we do."

She drew her hand from his grip. "We're not beasts." She tried not to think of her brother's missing heart.

Jorn captured her hand again. "I can feel more than pain when I'm in contact with you. Why does that bother you?"

"Survival of the fittest. We come from a volatile world and the world we prefer to hunt in is even more volatile with Viking raiders and other races who live for the fight."

"How do you know? You were born in this world."

She shared images with him. Ones given to her by Gilda and others she'd caught glimpses of when she'd been practising how to push past people's mental barriers. "My grandfather had all his children, grandchildren and great-grandchildren wiped out at one stage. When my mother was born, he locked her safely away to ensure that no matter what happened to the other children he had, there would always be someone left of his bloodline to carry it on."

"Then why is she here?" Jorn asked.

"As she puts it, she fell in love with a handsome face and a charming personality. My grandfather thought this place would be safe since dragons hadn't come here before." A wry smile formed. "Then something changed. Brigitte swears it was her father's doing, locking this world away from the others, Gilda believes something else occurred. That as powerful as their family is, they weren't capable of this."

"There's been a lot of debate amongst the older hunters about what it meant when the world closed in upon itself. There were some who could travel through a Void. And occasionally creatures of pure energy visited. There were also the fierce ones that could take on the shape of another. We haven't missed them. Most believe it's a good thing the world closed in upon itself. For now, it's ours and more of your people can't follow."

Morgane started to protest that they wouldn't have followed, but she left the words unspoken. They were dragons. They wanted to conquer everything they saw. Even she had a hoard she'd shared with her brother, hidden away in the forest. Gold and jewels and various trinkets they'd managed to gain over the years.

Jorn frowned. "Pleasure? Or satisfaction?"

"You made me think of other times. Of when my brother lived."

"We've always been taught that dragons don't care for anyone but themselves. You do. Deeply."

"Not all dragons do. Some can't see beyond their own desires."

"What makes you different?"

She didn't know that she was different from other dragons. She'd only ever known those who'd been left behind in this world, most of them pining for the life they'd once had. But if she was different, she had a theory even though she had no way of proving it. "I was raised in this world." Unlike some of the others who'd been born here, she didn't pine for another world.

He studied her for a moment before inclining his head. "When are we going after a dragon for your experiments?"

"I need time to prepare some things. Can you take Cort away from here so neither of you see what I'm doing?"

He didn't answer immediately. "I'll suggest scouting the area." He rose to his feet, taking a step towards the exit.

She was in front of him in a flash of movement. "No questions?"

"If you tell me exactly what the ingredient is, I'll have to share it with Tarben. I'm not sure I want to do that." He held her gaze a moment before he strode outside.

She stared after him, confusion washing over her. He was meant to be her enemy. Why didn't he want to learn all her secrets? She'd expected to have to argue the need for the two of them to leave her alone. Trying to hear what Jorn said to Cort, she resorted to dragon bone.

"We wouldn't need to scout the area if we captured her instead," Cort said.

"Did you not hear me the first time? I said no. You made a deal with her. Where is your honour?"

"The deal wasn't to never harm her. She's a dragon. Where is your honour?"

Morgane tensed, her hand going to her dagger.

"I owe her a life debt," Jorn said.

"Then pay it back so we can capture her and not need to go after another one. This is a waste of time when we already have a dragon," Cort said.

Jorn didn't answer immediately. "If you attack her, you also attack me."

"She can't be family. She's a dragon. A beast that eats humans."

"My sister and cousin claim her family of the heart. You attack her, you attack me," Jorn stated.

"Does she feel the same way?" Cort asked.

"She claims my sister and cousin as the family of her heart."

"You going to tell her about this discussion?" Cort asked.

"That won't be necessary."

Morgane relaxed at hearing the humour in Jorn's tone.

"Why do you find that so amusing?" Cort demanded.

"We need to scout the area. Make sure it's safe. See if there's anyone nearby or any warning signs left by hunters."

Morgane remained where she was, listening to their voices move further away. Had that been the real reason Jorn had protected her? Owing her a life debt and the way his family felt about her. Or was it because he guessed she could hear what they said even though both had kept their voices low? She had no idea and only time would tell. Straightening her shoulders, she forced herself to return to the task of removing bone from the dragons. She focused on her brother first, not wanting to leave his body lying around any longer than necessary.

By the time Jorn and Cort returned late in the afternoon, she had all the bones she planned to remove from her brother's corpse stacked at the back of the cave. She'd also collected rocks to cover them with in an attempt at keeping creatures from gnawing on them. It was heartbreaking to see what was left of her brother's corpse and she kept having to force herself to continue. He would want Elin and Anja protected too. He might not have met them, but they'd been important to him because they'd meant so much to her. Even while he feared what might happen to her because she associated with them, he'd continued to make it possible for her to sneak away from the castle.

While they'd been gone, she'd removed a couple of bones from the warrior, smaller ones that she'd shaved and dried by the fire, grinding them up. She'd added some of the ground bone to the deer fat, mixing it into a paste and gathering broad, long grasses to wrap it into parcels.

Cort stared at the dismembered dragon. "Why did you do this?"

She hadn't bothered to wash the dried blood from her arms, having rolled her sleeves up earlier. "These remains have to be taken to the funeral pyre." She looked down at what was left of her brother, breathing in deeply as she fought against the pain. "Only this one. We'll deal with the other one later."

Jorn moved forward to rest a hand on her shoulder. "We can do this for you if you wish."

She met his gaze, surprised by the compassion she

could see in his dark eyes. "I need to do this." She couldn't desert her brother's remains to those who hadn't known him.

Jorn momentarily tightened his grip on her shoulder before letting go and facing the corpse. "I spotted some fan palm trees further along the river. We can cut some of them and plait the fronds together to make large grass bowls to carry some of this."

Cort continued to stare at the bloody mess. "This isn't the sort of experimenting you're planning on doing to the dragon we're going to catch, is it?"

"I offered you a live dragon." Morgane gestured towards the bodies. "Do these look alive to you?"

"Well no, but-"

Jorn interrupted Cort. "You and I will deal with the fan palms."

"Now wait-"

Once more Jorn interrupted him. "Surely you're capable of that."

"That's not what I-"

"Then let's get moving." Jorn ushered him towards the river, interrupting his protests.

Morgane sank to the ground, first checking it was free of blood. She stared at her stained hands and arms. How was she going to survive without

Gwynham in her life? How was she going to survive without anyone at all in her life?

"Morgane?" There was a thread of worry in Jorn's thoughts.

"I'm all right."

"Are you certain? I felt your pain from beside the river."

She nearly didn't answer him. *"I have no people."* Jorn didn't answer, but she felt his presence with her for a moment longer.

While they were gone, she continued to remove bones from the warrior, hiding them behind the pile of rocks she'd used to cover her brother's bones. She hadn't got much done by the time they returned. Being able to sense them coming allowed her to hide the signs of what she'd been doing. She almost smiled when Cort's attention was focused on her bloody hands.

By the time they'd taken Gwynham's remains to the funeral pyre, and lit it, the sun was sinking and the forest was full of shadows. She watched as the smoke rose into the sky, holding back the tears that wanted to fall. It seemed too final. He'd always been in her life. Even when they were apart, she'd known he was there. Now he wasn't.

Jorn stepped close, his arm pressing against hers.

"They never really go. Not the family of our heart. They remain in our hearts forever."

She gave a single nod, relieved he'd spoken the words directly to her so Cort didn't hear them. The last thing she wanted to do was explain anything to him. Especially since he'd rather take her back than capture another dragon.

"How long are we meant to stay here?" Cort asked.

She stared into the flames. "Until there's nothing left."

"I can use my magic to speed it along," Cort offered.

Jorn slipped his hand in hers. "When someone leaves this world, surely those left behind can spare them a little time without wanting to rush off and do other things."

Cort gestured towards the pyre. "That was a dragon."

"That was once a living, breathing being," Jorn stated.

Cort looked past Morgane to Jorn. "This dragon was also your friend?"

"I never met him." Jorn momentarily tightened his grip on Morgane's hand. "That doesn't mean I can't appreciate that there are some who will miss him."

"Two," Morgane said softly. "Only two will miss him."

"That doesn't say much about someone when so few will miss him," Cort said.

Anger rushed through Morgane and she faced Cort, tugging her hand from Jorn's grip. "It says a great deal about a dragon when there are actually some who will mourn his passing. Mostly, when a dragon dies, those left behind think only of revenge, not what they've lost."

Cort took a step back from her. "He was a dragon." His words were uncertain.

"Yes." She took a step towards Cort, brought up short when Jorn grabbed hold of her shoulder. She spoke directly in his mind. *"Let go of me."*

"You made a promise," Jorn thought to her.

"I have no plans to break it. Now, let go of me."

Jorn lowered his hand. "If you don't want to remain with us while the pyre is burning, Cort, why not scout the area?"

"We did that earlier and there was nothing to see," Cort said.

"Then stay here, but remain silent." Jorn moved to stand shoulder to shoulder with Morgane again.

Cort looked from one to the other. "I never thought I'd see one of our people side with a dragon."

He strode away, sitting on a rock at the base of a tree, leaning back against the trunk.

Chapter Thirteen

Morgane stared at Cort a moment longer before she faced the pyre. *"Thank you."* She sent the words directly to Jorn.

"Don't thank me. I would respect the savages' right to bury their dead and mourn them. All deserve that courtesy. We aren't beasts."

She didn't comment, remaining beside him as she guarded her brother's pyre, letting the pain wash over her along with the memories. With Cort well behind her, she allowed the tears to fall, grateful when Jorn again took hold of her hand. If she ever managed to spend time with Elin again, she'd refrain from teasing her when she praised Jorn for the things he'd done. It was quite possible her friend's case of hero worship for her older brother wasn't misplaced.

The fire had nearly burned down when Morgane heard a disturbance in the direction of the cave. Her hand started to go to the belt pouch, but she stopped. There was no way she could have some of the bone in front of Cort. Or even Jorn. He was still her enemy even though he'd offered his comfort for her loss. She couldn't lower her defences to a point where she forgot that. Straining to hear, she was unable to figure out exactly what was happening.

"Is something wrong?" Jorn asked.

"There's a disturbance at the cave."

Jorn glanced in the direction they'd come from. "We'll have a look. You remain here to the end."

She inclined her head, her hand feeling cold when he let go to stride over to Cort. She listened to them speak, the two of them heading back to the cave, readying their weapons. As soon as they were out of sight, or rather too far for her to sense, she took the dragon bone from her belt pouch and had a piece. Energy rushed through her and her hearing improved. Along with her other abilities. It took her a moment to realise what she heard. Russet cave bears. They tore apart the dragon warrior that had been left outside the cave, easily snapping bones and stripping flesh away with their sharp claws.

Closing her eyes she focused on figuring out how many. For a moment she thought there was only two, then she heard the rumble as more raced through the forest, answering the call of their pack. Five more ran towards the cave. There was no way two hunters could survive seven russet cave bears. Even a dragon would struggle to take on so many. And who knew what eating a dragon warrior would do to them.

"I'm sorry." She whispered the words to her brother, tugging a few strands of her hair out from under the dragon-leather scarf. The white strands caught the colour of the fire and she pulled a couple from her head, tossing them into the fire. "I won't let another blood brother or blood sister be used like you."

She placed another few bits of dragon bone in her mouth before racing through the forest, expertly avoiding trees as she moved at a speed she hadn't been able to accomplish yesterday. She arrived in the clearing, stopping in front of the cave entrance at the same time as the hunters and second lot of russet cave bears arrived.

Sensing Cort head for a tree, she glanced in his direction, readying her bow. "They can climb. Better than you. They can also smell you while you're invisible. No matter how hard you try to hide your scent." She drew back an arrow, firing it at the closest bear.

The creature roared, rising on hind legs, long fangs

catching the moonlight, claws dripping blood, flesh clinging to them. It bounded towards her, not slowed by the arrows that sank into its shaggy body.

Slipping the bow across her back and latching the lid of her quiver, she drew her dagger, leaping across the bear as it came for her, slashing at him as she did so. Landing on the ground, she spun to face the bear that was already turning towards her. "Cort! Get out of the tree." She raced at the closest bear, hearing more behind her. "One of them has your scent. Run for the river if all you plan to do is hide."

She leapt on the bear again, narrowly missing the arrows Jorn fired into it, sinking the dagger into the shaggy coat before drawing it out as she continued past the bear to land on the ground. There was no time to attack it again. Avoiding two bears, she ran for the one that climbed up the tree after Cort. Leaping, she wrapped an arm around it, sinking the dagger into the throat. Warm blood poured over her hand and she threw herself from the bear that tried to twist around and attack her, taking the dagger with her.

Landing on the ground in a crouch, she barely had any time to assess the situation before she had to dodge another bear. The one that had been climbing after Cort thudded to the ground, struggling to rise.

An arrow sank into it as she turned to fend off another bear.

One down and already she was noticing a reduction in her energy. They needed to take out the other six a lot faster than they'd taken out the first one. She leapt on the back of another bear, but had no chance to do anything as a second bear came in for the attack.

She heard the heartbeat of a bear slow and focused her attention on it. When a bear came to defend the dying creature, she leapt for the nearest tree, crouching on a low branch, checking both Jorn and Cort's whereabouts. There was too much blood to tell if any of it was theirs.

"Bear coming up your tree," Jorn warned.

"I know." She waited until it was close before she dropped onto it, sinking the dagger into the throat before leaping for another bear on the ground. Her energy ebbed further and she barely managed to avoid sharp claws. There was no time to eat dragon bone. If it wasn't for the bracelet she would have been able to fly the bears into the air and drop them from a great height. The image of Jorn raising the warrior off the ground came to her.

She leapt for another tree, feeling the air from a

swipe aimed at her. "Jorn, how far can you lift one of these creatures into the air?"

"Not high enough for the fall to kill it." Jorn fired an arrow into the bear that bounded after her.

"I can help," Cort offered. "Focus on that one." He fired an arrow into a bear coming towards his tree.

"Keep the rest off us, Morgane," Jorn said.

"Then throw me your dagger." She leapt from the tree, grabbing the weapon from mid-air to drop onto a bear below her, sinking both daggers into it and immediately drawing them out. She was moving to another bear before that one could do anything.

"Watch out," Jorn called a moment before a bear plummeted from the sky.

She shoved another bear out of the way, not wanting to risk it breaking the falling bear's landing. The thud as it hit the ground could be felt beneath her feet. "Take this one." She leapt over the one that tried to attack her, finishing off the one that had hit the ground, it's feeble heartbeat ending after she drew the dagger from it.

Turning, she saw a bear bounding towards Jorn. Leaping for it, she nearly missed as her energy dropped further. The bear tossed her to the ground and she landed hard, the air forced from her lungs.

"Morgane!" A thud followed Jorn's call

A rush of air washed over her and she struggled to her feet in time to see the bear knocked backwards. She sensed Jorn close behind her.

"What happened?" Jorn sent the words directly to her.

She spoke with her mind when she answered. *"Losing energy fast."*

He wrapped a hand around her bracelet. *"We're nearly done."*

The metal warmed against her skin and energy crackled through her. With a nod, she ran for the closest bear, that Cort was valiantly trying to keep from them with gusts of air. She had no idea how much longer he could keep it up, but it must have been difficult for him since he was no longer invisible.

Leaping on the back of a bear that struggled to rise, she sank the daggers into its neck, drawing them out and leaping for another one before it could swipe at her. It seemed like barely a heartbeat before another bear thudded to the ground and she finished it off, the rest going the same way, kept from Jorn and Cort by her leaps and attacks.

Standing amongst the seven bodies, she wiped her dagger along the leg of her trousers before she sheathed it. Again exhaustion tugged at her.

Jorn came to stand beside her, taking his dagger from her. "You look like you could do with a dip in the river."

"At this time of the night? It'll be freezing."

"What do you plan to do with the blood then? Lick it off?" Cort joined them, gathering what arrows were salvageable.

"What do you think we are? Some kind of cat?" Morgane demanded.

"Dragons like blood. You drank my blood so you can't say you don't like it." Cort slung his bow across his back, having a drink from the waterskin hanging at his side.

Morgane took a step towards him, anger rushing through her.

Jorn drew her back with a hand on her shoulder. "No one eats russet cave bears. Not even a dragon. They taste disgusting. Why would a dragon eat something so revolting when there's freshly cooked venison?"

"What are we going to do with them? They'll draw more creatures in." Cort took another drink from his waterskin before hanging it at his side.

"Take them further up river. It might draw creatures there instead of here." Jorn glanced at the warrior the bears had torn apart. "Although why anything would choose them over a dragon I haven't a clue."

"I need to return to the funeral pyre." Morgane took a step in that direction.

Jorn tugged her back to him. "I'll go with you. Let me help Cort move these bodies first. Why not wash your hands and arms before you return."

She started to argue, catching a look in his eyes that she didn't understand. Not wanting to ask him in front of Cort, she nodded and headed for the river. Once she'd washed the blood from her hands, arms and face, shivering at the coldness of the water, she had some of the dragon bone before she returned to the cave. Neither Jorn nor Cort were there. It didn't take her long to sense them. They were moving towards the cave. A glance around the area showed all the bears were gone. Although now there was more blood soaking into the ground of the clearing.

Jorn stepped into the clearing, Cort behind him. "You waited."

She nodded, the surprise in his tone causing yet one more question she'd like answered.

"You don't expect me to stay here on my own with that to call more creatures in." Cort gestured towards the dragon warrior.

A sigh escaped as she looked from the warrior to

Cort. "Come with us if you must." She strode through the forest, Jorn at her side, Cort following with a ball of light in his hand. She wanted to tell him to put it out. He didn't need to draw the attention of anyone who might be in the area. But she supposed having him crash around in the forest would be as bad and anyone in the area had probably already noticed the fire.

Reaching the pyre, she was relieved Cort returned to the same rock he'd sat on before, putting the light out once he was seated. The flames of the fire were mostly out, only a few still burning in the centre. Bending, she placed her hands on the ashes at the outer edge. They were warm, yet cool enough she could touch them.

Scooping up two handfuls, she rubbed them into her arms, trying to ignore the hunters with her. It was a little difficult since she could sense them no matter where they stood and more than impossible considering Jorn was at her side. Blocking out all distractions, she ran the ashes over her arms and rubbed them into her hands, staring at the flames that were dying out. There should have been others here to do the same. Others to speak the ceremonial words each clan member would normally say. "You will always be a part of me. You will live on through the actions of the clan." She scooped up more ashes, rubbing them across her cheeks. "Gwynham." Her words were soft. She would have prefered to keep them to herself and not share them. As the last flame flickered out, she scooped up one more lot of ashes, raising them to her lips, her forehead then her heart. Scattering them on the wind, she walked away, Jorn's presence in her mind.

Cort started to speak, but Jorn interrupted him, telling him to hush.

Instead of thanking Jorn, she sent a wave of gratitude through their link, relieved he didn't answer. She wanted the silence, wanted to let her thoughts drift for a moment. The morning would be here soon enough. Her plotting and planning to take down the dragons could wait until then. She was a dragon. No matter what Brigitte had said over the years. A fierceness rushed through her. And no matter what she did to try and prevent her from being a dragon, it wouldn't change anything. She was a dragon. And if she wanted the chance to survive in this world, she needed to act like one, not wallow in her grief like a human. Letting those who'd hurt her, or one of hers, to get away with it unharmed would have all the dragons seeing her as weak. Only the strong survived.

The feel of the ash against her skin reminded her of Jorn's earlier words. Gwynham would always be a part of her. His death hadn't changed that. But it had changed other things. If she didn't want to join him in death she needed to find a way to show she was strong without killing Brigitte. That was one thing she knew she wasn't capable of. Helping the villagers wouldn't be enough. She had to be seen doing something to avenge the death of her brother.

Cort, who followed, a ball of light in his hands again, tried to speak. "What–"

Jorn interrupted. "Quiet."

"But–" Cort tried again.

Once more Jorn interrupted. "Later."

Chapter Fourteen

Morgane glanced at Jorn, who continued to stride at her side. It would be easy to become accustomed to him beside her. Drawing in a deep, slow breath she tried not to dwell on what her life would be like once she'd given dragon bone to the villagers and a live dragon to Cort. She couldn't let it stop her. She glanced at him again, this time noticing he glanced at her. Questions filled her mind. She pushed them away. Maybe it would be better not to know the answers. To keep her distance. She had a feeling it might already be too late.

Reaching the cave, Morgane checked everything was untouched and no other wild animals had entered while they were gone. The cave was empty of life and only a single scavenger had ventured close to the remains of the warrior. Grabbing her bow, Morgane shot it before it could escape into the forest.

"Are all dragons so fast?" Cort asked.

When Jorn started to hush him again, Morgane gestured for him to stop. She met Cort's gaze. "I'm slow in comparison to other dragons." She'd once been fast. Returning her bow to her back, and latching the lid of her quiver back down, she couldn't help running her fingers across the bracelet. "Are you sure you want to capture one?"

"I'm the youngest in a line of fourteen hunters. My deeds have to be greater than any of theirs if I'm to be taken seriously," Cort said.

"Your ancestors?" She started to ask what his ancestors had been before they'd become hunters.

Jorn interrupted. "His siblings."

She stared at him. "That is a lot of competition to beat."

Cort frowned. "It's not that I'm trying to beat them. Or that they're my competitors. It's…" His voice trailed off.

"He probably crept out of the village while his family slept, leaving a message so they didn't try and stop him from putting himself in danger," Jorn said.

Morgane looked from one to the other. "I still don't understand."

"They're protective. One or two is all right, but

when you have so many to look after you, it becomes smothering," Cort said.

"You're important in some way?" Morgane asked.

"Don't your family try and protect you when you're young, sometimes not realising you're old enough to protect yourself?" Jorn asked.

She shook her head. "We wake to poisonous snakes in our bed if we sleep too heavy, we're thrown off cliffs when we're toddlers and are expected to shapeshift before we hit the ground and once we begin to train in the use of a sword, we have people attack us at random times of the day and night."

She could feel Jorn's shock and it had been impossible to miss noticing his involuntary movement towards her.

"Your family try to kill you?" Cort demanded.

"No. They teach us that only the strong survive." She studied Cort, surprised to find he was as shocked as Jorn. "Why does this bother the two of you?"

"Why doesn't it bother you?" Jorn asked.

"It's the way it's always been." There'd only been one dragon she could completely trust and now he was ashes and a pile of bones hidden in the back of a cave. She gestured towards the campfire, wanting to end the uncomfortable conversation. "I'll gather more wood." She sidestepped Jorn when he tried to stop her. Walking off didn't stop him from sending her his thoughts.

"This is why you're friends with Elin and Anja."

She didn't bother to comment, picking up several branches, moving further away from the cave.

"They're the only ones to treat you like a human."

"I'm a dragon. We don't need to be treated like a human." She continued to fill her arms with branches.

"Yet I think you do."

Gathering two more branches, she headed back to the cave, dumping them by the campfire. She faced Jorn who'd come close, Cort remaining outside the cave. "No. I don't. That will lead to being weak when one needs to be strong."

"There can be strength in weakness."

"How?"

"You can be both weakened and strengthened by your ties to others."

She had no idea how to reply and was relieved when she sensed Cort coming towards the cave. Taking a step back from Jorn, she looked in Cort's direction. "Did you want something?"

"To hunt down a dragon."

She gestured to the parcels of fat and bone paste. "Tomorrow. We'll go after one tomorrow."

"That is the ingredient?" Jorn picked up one of the parcels, opening it to smell the contents.

When he started to dip his finger in it, she swatted his hand away. "Don't taste it. I don't know what it'll do to a human." She knew dragon blood and dragon bone taken too close together could weaken a human, but had no idea if that held true here or was the same for the humans of this world.

"What is it?" Cort peered closely at it, also smelling the paste.

"Something that should weaken a dragon." She nodded to the venison that had been cooked earlier. "Food and then sleep. I'll take first watch." She'd finish sorting the bones of the warrior while she watched for intruders. Leaving the remains behind would draw in creatures that might find the bones in the back of the cave.

After they'd eaten, Morgane paced outside as she waited for them to fall asleep so she could finish with the remains. It took her longer than expected and she carefully stacked the bones in a hollow outside the cave, covering them with rocks in the hope no creature would find them. Tired, and well past the time she was meant to keep watch, she woke Jorn, going to the river to wash once he was awake.

When she returned, Jorn stepped in front of her,

preventing her from entering the cave. He nodded towards the remains. "What were you doing with him?"

"I can't tell you."

"I can guess from what I saw of your brother and what I can see of this one."

"We need to burn his remains. It should be done before we leave tomorrow. But not too close to the cave. We don't want anyone to find it. We'll need somewhere to return to with the dragon." She tried to push past Jorn.

He stepped in front of her. "I'm sorry for all you endured as a child."

"Don't be. That's the way our society is. To treat us like a human would result in our death. Only the fittest survive." This time she was able to push past him and enter the cave. She picked up her cloak and found a spot well away from Cort and close to the bones.

Cort half sat up. "Is it my turn?"

"No. Go back to sleep. Jorn is keeping watch." She wrapped the cloak around herself and lay down.

"What was it like?" Cort asked softly.

"What are you asking about?"

"Growing up always expecting someone to kill you."

She didn't bother correcting him that it hadn't been all the time. Nor had it been everyone. Gwynham and Gilda had never attempted to kill her. "Full of meaningful triumphs."

"That makes a strange kind of sense."

"Go to sleep. We have a lot to do come morning." She closed her eyes, listening to Cort's breathing slow, all the time aware of where Jorn was.

Her sleep was dreamless and she woke before Jorn could reach her, aware of him moving close to her. She stared up at him, the grey of dawn silhouetting him. "It's time to rise?"

Jorn nodded.

Cort sat up. "What happened to my turn at keeping watch?"

"You'll have to ask Morgane." Jorn gestured towards the campfire. "I've sliced some venison thin and placed rocks amongst the coals to cook it. Shouldn't take too long to cook and then we can figure out our plan."

Morgane rose to her feet, keeping the cloak around her. She needed to have more dragon bone. The cold was seeping into her body, something it didn't normally do.

Over their morning meal, they argued out their plan. Jorn wanted to involve some of the people from his village. Morgane and Cort didn't. Both for different reasons. Morgane didn't want anyone to know what she planned to do with the dragon afterwards, testing it with different dragon bone amounts, and Cort didn't want to risk them taking the dragon from him.

Eventually, they agreed they'd capture the dragon on their own and tidied up the area, including creating another pyre in a different clearing to the one they'd used yesterday. They didn't stay to watch it burn down.

After cleaning her hands in the river, Morgane strode ahead of the two hunters, taking a piece of the dragon bone she'd left loose in the bottom of her belt pouch and popping it in her mouth before either of them could catch up to her. She brushed her fingers across the belt pouch, thinking of the various contents. Her brother's hair, the other lot of dragon bone, the paste of bone and fat and cooked slices of venison. She'd left her rucksack in the cave, hidden behind the bones at the back, but had brought her weapons with her. It wasn't a lot, but hopefully she had enough gear to capture a dragon.

By the middle of the day, they were hidden behind the castle, peering out of the forest as they ate the venison for their midday meal. Several human women were washing clothes in the pond, talking and laughing as they went about their work.

"I thought they'd have dragon guards," Cort said.

"Why would they need guards?" Morgane asked. "Who'd be crazy enough to come this close and attack during the day, other than us?"

"No, to keep them from escaping." Cort gestured towards the women.

Morgane frowned, his words not making sense. "Why would they want to escape?"

"From the dragons," Cort said.

Jorn laughed softly.

Cort looked from one to the other. "I didn't say anything at all amusing."

"It's clear you're not from around here," Jorn said. "They're happy to work for the dragons. Some prefer to live in a castle and not have to worry about anything other than serving Brigitte."

"But she's a monster," Cort exclaimed.

"She's my mother," Morgane said.

"Uhm, I…" Cort's voice trailed off.

Jorn laughed softly again. "Things are never completely right or wrong."

Movement caught Morgane's attention. Two dragon warriors strode towards the pond, swords at their sides, rucksacks made of dragon-leather at their back. Morgane's jaw tightened. "Him. We take him down." She pointed to the one on the left. "Him we capture." She pointed to the one on the right, trying not to think of how he'd been one of the warriors who'd practised with her and Gwynham when they'd been learning how to use a sword.

"Why do we want him?" Cort asked.

"Becan has Gold in his ancestry." The stronger the bloodline, the more accurate her results should be. Or at least that's what she tried to tell herself. Capturing him would give him the chance to escape before Cort reached his village. Three days worth of chances.

"What about the other one?" Jorn asked.

Morgane looked him up and down. She had no good memories of him. Only assassination attempts. Ones sanctioned by Brigitte. "Kill him."

"Just like that? You have no qualms about killing one of your own people?" Cort demanded.

"Would you have qualms about killing someone who'd thrown you off a cliff?"

Jorn readied his bow. "We kill him."

Cort nodded. "What about the other one?"

"We trained with him. He's really good with a sword even though he's only a few years older than me." Morgane dipped two arrows into the paste. "Distract them. Fire at the one on the left first. At the same time. On two. Then the same for Becan. Only don't aim for anything vital."

Cort drew back his arrow. "Ready."

"Start counting." Jorn aimed at the warrior.

"One, two." She let go of the string of her bow a fraction of a heartbeat after they let go of theirs, the second arrow already being drawn back. "One, two." Again she fired after them. The first warrior turned into a dragon, his body collapsing on the ground, an arrow in his heart, two arrows lying on the ground where he'd knocked them. Becan spun to run towards the castle, the women shouting that they were under attack.

"Shoot him again?" Cort drew back an arrow.

"No." Morgane gave the paste to Jorn. She had more in her belt pouch if she needed it. "Legs and arms only."

Chapter Fifteen

Slinging her bow onto her back and latching her quiver shut, Morgane raced towards the warrior, the women streaming past him to the castle, their washing discarded by the water's edge.

"What are you doing?" Jorn thought to her.

"Someone has to collect Becan," she thought back to him.

"It doesn't have to be you."

She slipped her hand into her belt pouch, taking out another piece of the dragon bone lying in the bottom. Energy rushed through her the moment she consumed it and she ran faster, catching up to Becan who was struck in the leg by an arrow. She tackled him to the ground, yanking his hands above his head, pressing a dagger to his throat. "Come quietly and today doesn't have to be the one when you die."

"What did you do to me, Morgane? What was on your arrow?"

She dragged him to his feet. "Do you promise to come quietly?" She tugged him towards the forest, hearing movement from the direction of the castle. They wouldn't have much time.

"Why would I make a promise like that? If I have the opportunity, I will run."

"Give me your promise you'll remain with us until the sun sets or I'll be forced to end your life." Morgane kept her dagger pressed against his throat, wishing he wasn't so much taller and broader than her.

"Only if you give me your promise I'll live to see the sun rise," Becan said.

"Done."

Becan pushed her hand that held the dagger away from his throat. "I give you my word."

She grabbed hold of his hand, running towards the forest with him. "Can't you go faster than this?"

"Not with what you used on me. I doubt I could turn into a dragon right now either."

She grinned. "That's good to hear."

"What did you use?" Becan asked as they reached the treeline.

"What's going on?" Cort gestured towards Morgane's hand in Becan's.

"We've reached a temporary agreement." Morgane glanced over her shoulder. Dragons took flight, heading towards where they hid. "We don't kill him before sunrise and he comes with us until sunset."

"Then we better start moving." Jorn put the paste in his belt pouch and his bow on his back. "Does that include him not letting any warriors know where he's hiding?"

"It does," Morgane said. "Now get moving. We'll be surrounded shortly."

Jorn tugged Becan from her. "We'll hide. I'll take this one and Cort can hide you."

"I never agreed to anything with you." Becan tried to pull away from Jorn's grip.

She met Becan's blue eyes. His blond hair had once been as fair as hers and Gwynham's, but it had darkened as he'd grown older. "He'll abide by the terms. You can trust his word."

Becan barely managed to nod before he and Jorn vanished from sight.

Cort grabbed Morgane's hand and tugged her close. "Don't make a sound."

The light bent around them and she stepped lightly when he drew her against a tree. She should have given him her blood so she could talk to him in his mind. She sensed Jorn moving further away from the castle. How was she meant to tell Cort they needed to move in that direction? If she drew her dagger, he'd think she was about to attack him.

A dragon warrior walked past them, within arm's reach. "They can't have gone too far."

Morgane held her breath, not daring to move. How good was Cort at hiding? How long would his magic last? She needed to know. Biting her lip, she turned to press her lips against Cort's, seeing a moment of surprise in his eyes before he started to pull away. It was too late. She grinned, reaching for his mind. *"It seemed safer than drawing my dagger to cut myself."*

Cort wiped the back of a hand across his mouth, keeping hold of her with the other. *"Why did you kiss me?"*

"You kissed him?" Jorn demanded.

"How else was I meant to give him my blood?" Morgane hadn't realised Jorn would hear too. Had thought she could only sense his presence, not his mind. *"I couldn't exactly draw my dagger."*

"Get out of my head," Cort ordered. *"I didn't give you permission."*

"What about the dragon? Can he hear us?" Jorn asked.

"He should be able to." Morgane watched as another warrior came close. *"Did you want me to bring him into the conversation?"*

"Not particularly, but I think he wants to tell me something. He keeps looking at me like he has something to say," Jorn said.

"Hold on then." Morgane reached for Becan's mind, drawing him into the conversation. *"Did you want to tell Jorn something?"*

"You've given him your blood?"

"Both of them and you better not take any blood from us," Morgane warned even though she didn't know if he had that ability. It was bad enough Brigitte could sense her through her blood. She didn't need other dragons able to track any of them down. Track her down. She wouldn't always have Jorn or Cort at her side.

"Take none of mine and I'll take none from any of you," Becan said. *"And it might be best if we moved away from this area. Whatever you used on me doesn't agree with me and I might very well be throwing up soon."*

"Start moving towards the cave." Morgane waited until a warrior had moved away from them before she tugged Cort towards Jorn. *"The sooner-"* She broke off, hushing her companions when they tried to ask

what was wrong. *"Stay out of my head, Brigitte is trying to reach me."* There was no way she could hold her off for long. She wasn't strong enough. Although she'd managed for longer than usual. Her fingers brushed across the belt pouch and she wondered if it was due to the bone. Pushing all thoughts from her mind, she lowered her defences. *"What do you want?"*

"I've sent Dorran after you. I can sense exactly where you are and will be able to lead him directly to you."

Somehow she managed to keep her emotions in check. *"Why not come after me yourself? Or are you afraid you might fail?"*

"You are a hatchling, compared to me, when it comes to experience. Can you see him coming towards you? Not long now and you'll be back in the castle where you belong. If this next child isn't Gold, your heart will be mine. I have no other use for you after what you've done. If it wasn't for your father, I wouldn't be stuck in this world."

"Not meeting him wouldn't have made a difference. If you weren't left here you would still have been imprisoned in your father's castle as a surety against fate." Morgane wrenched her mind from Brigitte's conversation, mentally gathering her companions. *"They can track me. Or at least Brigitte can and she's sent Dorran after me. I'll lead him away while the rest of you return to*

the cave. I'll meet you there. Help them communicate with each other Becan and I'll promise to keep you alive until the middle of the day tomorrow."

"Don't–"

She pushed them from her mind before Jorn could finish his comment, pulling from Cort's light grip. There was no time for arguments. Dorran strode through the trees towards her. She ran through the forest, angling away from her companions, hearing pursuit behind her. More than Dorran followed. She was going to need dragon bone. She should have left more loose in the belt pouch.

Behind her branches broke. The warriors didn't try to hide they were coming after her. The sounds came closer, reducing the distance between them. She tried to run faster. Her energy was rapidly dwindling. She needed more dragon bone. Fumbling at her belt pouch, she ended up finding the dragon bone paste, wincing at the mess she made in her belt pouch.

"Think you can outrun us?" Dorran called out.

Finding the leather wrapped parcel of dragon bone that she needed, she managed to get it open enough to have a few pieces stick to the fat smeared across her fingers. The moment she consumed them, energy burst through her and she picked up speed, coming out of the trees and into a clearing. Pushing herself, she ran towards the trees on the other side.

A rush of air came at her and she was grabbed around the waist, Dorran shooting into the air with her. He circled around, heading towards the castle, roaring triumphantly.

Plans ran through her mind, impractical and impossible plans. None were perfect. So she went with the best option. Drawing her dagger, she stabbed at his forearm, smearing the dragon bone paste into the wound.

Dorran faltered, trying to talk to her in her mind.

She pushed him from her mind, not interested in anything he had to say, smearing more dragon bone paste into the wound. If he fell from the sky, he'd take her with him, but at least she'd avoid being dragged back to the castle. Frowning, she realised Jorn had changed direction and was coming towards her instead of the cave. Cort continued in the direction of the cave. She had no idea where Becan was.

Dorran veered away from the castle and the warriors that flew ahead of him, aiming for a clearing below. He rapidly lost height.

Morgane readied herself for a bad landing, sheathing her dagger so she didn't risk stabbing herself. The ground came up fast and she wrenched herself from Dorran's grip, grabbing the branch of a tree he flew above as he aimed for the clearing. She swung herself to the ground, landing on her feet, taking more dragon bone from her belt pouch. Striding towards Dorran, who was collapsed on the ground in human form, she licked the bone shavings from her fingers. A mixture of bone, fat and blood filled her senses and she was able to tell exactly where Dorran was. Even if he escaped she'd be able to find him.

Dorran staggered to his feet. "That's why you took the warrior. For the bone. To use it against us." He drew the sword that hung at his side.

Rage filled her. "That's Gwynham's sword."

Dorran's lips curved into a satisfied smile. "Brigitte gave it to me."

She drew her dagger. He was too close for her to use a bow. "Who killed him?" Behind her she sensed Jorn. Why was he coming towards her instead of going to the cave?

"Do you think she'd have given the task to another? I'm the one she relies on. The one she's asked to rule this world with her."

Her grip tightened on the dagger. "You won't live long enough to rule anything." She darted in, slicing his arm before he could block, darting back out of the way.

"I've called warriors to me. You haven't the time to kill me before they arrive." He attacked, driving her towards the trees.

She let him, preferring not to be in the open. "I'll tear your heart from you before they have the chance to reach you."

"Shall I tell you how his heart tasted?"

She focused on attacking, refusing to let his words get to her. "I'll tear your ribcage apart and rip your heart from your chest."

"You saw him. He screamed for you. In his last moments, you were the one he called for and you didn't come."

Pain shot through her and she stumbled.

An arrow flew past her, sinking into Dorran's shoulder. He staggered back, ripping it from his body. "You sided with the village?"

She kept her expression blank. "As if they'd side with me. It's an outcast. He hates all those at the castle as much as I do." She couldn't risk him telling Brigitte to go after the village. She'd kill everyone. Including Elin and Anja.

Another arrow pierced Dorran. He roared, ripping

it from his leg. The next arrow he knocked from the air.

"The dragons are close," Jorn thought to her.

"Shoot him in the heart." She feinted to the left.

Dorran blocked her, the arrow piercing his chest.

She slammed him against the ground, plunging her dagger beneath his ribs and slicing across his body.

"She'll kill you." Blood foamed at Dorran's mouth.

"She can try." Pulling out the dagger, she plunged her hand in under his ribs, tearing his heart from his chest. He changed beneath her and she tumbled off the draconic form, landing on her back in the grass.

Jorn appeared above her. Grabbing her wrist, he pulled her to her feet. "We have to go."

Chapter Sixteen

The light bent around Morgane and Jorn and she sheathed her dagger, collecting the sword that had fallen to the ground. She stumbled as she tried to keep up with Jorn, holding the heart against her chest. Pain exploded in her head and she struggled to keep Brigitte from her mind.

"What's happening?" Jorn staggered too, speaking the words aloud.

"Stay out of my head. Brigitte is trying to get in."

"How does she find you?" Jorn asked.

"She senses my blood."

"Is there a way for you to change it? Or to stop her?"

"Even in death the blood can be sensed." She tried to build up her defences. Brigitte pulled them down as quickly as she put them up.

Jorn slammed her against a tree, wrapping his arms

around her, the heart pressed between them. "Don't fight me. Stop fighting her. Accept."

She looked deep into his brown eyes, seeing her own pain mirrored back at her. "Run." She struggled to keep Brigitte from entering her mind.

"I can't. Not now." He closed his eyes, the light around them becoming brighter. He opened his eyes again, staring directly at her. "Trust me, Morgane. You're not alone in this world."

She relaxed against him, surrounded by the sense of him. "There are few I trust in this world and none in any other." She couldn't bring herself to beg him not to destroy her trust. What little of it she had.

The light around them brightened and his arms around her tightened, his gaze holding hers. "Your pain is my pain, your fight is my fight." His face came closer, a breath away. "My heart beats with your heart."

It felt like light exploded through her, tearing into her body, her mind, changing the pace of her heart. She let the pain fill her, let her defences crumble. Her sense of Jorn vanished, a different sense of him taking its place. In the back of her mind she heard Brigitte scream as she was forced from the connection. Catching her breath, Morgane asked softly, "What have you done?" She didn't know if she wanted him to answer.

"It's better if you don't know." He drew back slightly. "I expect nothing of you." He continued to hold her, the light bending around them. "I don't know how much longer I can keep us hidden. You might want to get rid of that heart so she can't use it to sense us."

She looked past him. Dragons landed in the clearing, changing form as they gathered around Dorran's body. A fierce joy raced through her. He'd killed her brother and she'd killed him.

"Leave the heart behind. I can't hide the smell of that much blood," Jorn thought to her.

"It's mine. Taken from my enemy. Taken from the one who killed my blood brother." She pressed it more firmly against her chest, the blood soaking through to her skin.

"We have to move." He took her hand as he stepped away from her, tugging her with him.

"Leave me behind. They can't find you." Her gaze was drawn to the blood smeared across his shirt. Unless Brigitte had taken blood from Dorran. Although she doubted he'd have let her. But it didn't hurt to take a few precautions. *"After you've washed in the river."*

"They can't find you either. After you leave the heart

behind." He kept moving through the forest, drawing her along with him.

She frowned. *"That doesn't make sense. Brigitte will always be able to sense me."*

"She can't find what no longer exists. Your signature has changed."

Still frowning, Morgane looked down at herself. *"I exist."*

Jorn glanced over his shoulder, smiling. *"We exist."*

Shock raced through her, the words reminding her of something Anja had once told her. About the words she never expected to hear since who would want to weaken themselves and connect to someone without magic. *"You married me? You bound our lives together?"*

"I should have known they'd tell you about it. And we don't marry. We bind our lives together with someone. A life partner or a hunting companion. We can only choose one."

She tugged against his hand that was wrapped around her wrist, weariness dragging at her. *"I'm a dragon. I can't be a hunter. Or a villager or use magic."* Why couldn't anyone understand who and what she was?

Jorn shrugged, keeping hold of her. *"The magic*

accepted us. I don't know what it'll mean, but we have changed. Our lives are bound." The light momentarily fractured around them before bending properly again.

"Can you turn into a dragon?"

"Can you?" He glanced at the bracelet on her wrist.

She felt a growl rumble up inside her, barely keeping it from escaping.

"We're going to have to stop bending the light around us. I don't want to weaken us." Again the light fractured momentarily.

"Weaken us?"

"Power and energy will ebb and flow when we're near each other. We don't have to be touching. In shouting distance." He glanced over his shoulder at her. *"Show me that again."*

"Show you what?"

He smiled. *"Your secrets are mine. I don't have to share them with the village."*

"Why did you do this?"

"Because you have no one and you don't deserve that. Nor do you deserve to be hunted by your mother."

"Pity?" She tried to pull from his grip.

"No. Admiration."

"That makes no sense." Behind them she heard

warriors searching, following them through the forest, her energy dwindling faster than usual.

"Prepare to fight. I need to let the light go. I can't keep drawing on your energy."

"You're stealing my energy?" She tried to pull away from him again.

"It's automatic. There's nothing I can do to prevent it. It'll take time for us to learn how to share equally."

A glance behind showed the warriors closing in. Too many for the two of them to face. She wasn't ready to die. There were things she needed to do. Like keep Elin and Anja safe. *"Take my sword and if you need to hold me to keep me invisible, then hold my arm up higher."*

He took the sword without question, shifting his grip on her.

"You promise this is between you and me?" She slipped her hand into her belt pouch. The contents were a mess.

"No one else. Our lives are entwined unless we make the journey to the sacred waters to have them ripped apart. Even then I'd keep your secrets gained during the time we're together. Honour demands it of me." He smiled down at her. *"But that isn't the reason I'd remain loyal to you."*

She wanted to ask him what the reason was, but there wasn't the time. Her fingers closed over what she hoped were the correct bone shavings and she raised them to her mouth. Energy burst through her, the light flaring around them. *"Enough or do you need more?"*

Jorn drew her to a stop, pulling her close to a tree. *"Where do we get more?"*

"You left it in the clearing and wanted me to throw away its heart."

"Dragon?"

She grinned at the confusion she could see in his expression. *"The bones of a Gold Dragon."*

"I wonder if they'd work for me. Or other hunters."

"This isn't for other hunters. Your people are powerful enough as it is."

"We need to go back for the body."

She started to tell him about Gwynham's bones, but they wouldn't last a lifetime at the rate she was consuming them.

"No, you're right. We need more than what you've stored in the cave."

"Get out of my head."

"I can't keep anything from you either. If you bothered to look." He smiled. *"No, it doesn't bother me. I have*

nothing to hide from you. Elin and Anja already shared most of the important things about our way of life."

"Learn some boundaries. You could if you chose to." She brought to mind learning how to become separate from her brother, their minds so entangled they'd nearly been one when they were hatchlings.

"That is simpler than what we're taught."

She felt Jorn's mind shift back slightly. *"Are we going after Dorran's body? It's still in the clearing. No one has moved it yet."* She supposed that was the priority. And likely the heart too. Which was why she couldn't understand how the warriors could walk right past them without noticing.

"We'll take the body back to the cave and process it there."

"What about Cort and Becan?"

"I'll take Cort scouting while you keep Becan from learning what we're doing." He headed in the direction they'd come from, his hand remaining high on her arm.

It felt strange making plans with someone when she'd expected a life of loneliness. But surely he wouldn't remain with her once all this was over. He'd mentioned they could undo what he'd done in the sacred waters. Had he told her that to let her know that was the plan once Elin and Anja were safe?

"You can't expect me to keep out of your thoughts when you're filled with pain."

"I expect you to keep out of my thoughts unless I invite you."

Jorn inclined his head. *"If that is what you wish."*

"It is." She glanced at him several times, but he didn't argue her words.

They strode through the forest, Morgane needing to have more dragon bone before they reached the edge of the clearing. Stepping out of cover, she half expected it to be a trap. Nothing happened. Even when they came close enough that Jorn linked his arm through hers so he could hold the sword with the hand that had been holding her arm and place the other hand on Dorran. The dragons who'd been sent after them had headed off in the wrong direction and none had been left to watch over Dorran's body.

Light bent around the dead dragon and he rose above the ground. *"Do we have enough dragon bone to get us back to the cave?"*

Morgane grinned. *"We have an entire corpse if we run out of the dragon bone in my belt pouch."* Or at least the dragon bone that was useful to her.

"We'll see how much it takes then." Jorn guided the body through the forest, having to skirt around the denser parts due to the bulky dragon hindering them.

They arrived back in front of the cave having to take a little bit of bone from Dorran. Jorn dumped the body where the previous warrior had been left. They'd barely taken two steps towards the cave, having become visible again, when Becan and Cort came out to meet them.

Becan stopped when he saw Dorran. "You killed him." His gaze went from the heart Morgane held then to the body, before returning to the heart. "He's dead."

Jorn stepped in front of Morgane. "Is that a problem?"

Morgane moved to Jorn's side. "He killed Gwynham." She took the sword from Jorn. "He deserved to die. It's a pity I could only kill him once."

Becan came close, stretching out his hand so he could touch the heart Morgane held. "If I hadn't sworn an oath to serve him, I would have killed him for what he did to my blood family."

Chapter Seventeen

Morgane frowned. "I thought your brother died from some mysterious sickness."

"He died after marrying a hunter. It isn't him who Dorran killed. It was their daughter. If I hadn't sworn an oath, along with my brother, to serve him as long as we remained in this world, I would have killed him."

"You would have only been two or three when you came here. How could he have made you swear such an oath?"

"Three. My brother had no one to leave me with. Dorran said if he was to let me accompany my brother, I had to make the same oath he did."

"What illness killed your brother?" Jorn asked. "I've heard of no plagues in this area in decades. The last one would have been before I was born."

Becan met Jorn's gaze a moment before he spoke.

"It was no plague." He faced Morgane. "You're the only Gold in this world I'd willingly serve."

"You don't need to serve anyone. This isn't our home world. Things are different here," Morgane said.

Cort joined them. "You promised him to me."

"I promised you a dragon. I didn't say for certain it'd be this one."

Cort's hand rested on his dagger. "You'd cheat me of what you promised?"

Jorn's hand also went to his dagger. "Nothing has changed. You'll have a dragon to take back to your village with you."

Becan dragged his gaze from the heart to meet Morgane's gaze. "You want a dragon? I'll bring one to you. Once I'm no longer weakened by what you used on me." Becan knelt in front of her, pressing his arms and upper body against the ground, looking up at her. "I would bring you Dorran's right hand warrior. The one that held my brother's daughter while Dorran wielded the sword. Neither believe there should be dragon and hunter pairings." He looked directly up at Morgane. "I know of no other way of life. I was raised to serve a Gold and one day we'll escape this world and return to that of our ancestors. I will remain at your side and serve you for as long as you have need of me."

"I know nothing of that world." Nor did she know if she wanted to go there even if the pathways between the worlds opened. She stared down at Becan. With him at her side, for as long as she had need of him, would mean she wouldn't have to worry about being alone once Elin and Anja were safe. The thought didn't bring the relief it should have and she barely managed to prevent herself from looking in Jorn's direction. "I haven't been raised to be a true Gold." Her gaze was momentarily drawn to the heart she held. "I have a feeling that after the first handful of years I was raised to live and survive only so I could provide more centuries for Brigitte."

"I would rather serve you than Brigitte." Becan remained at her feet.

"Don't trust him. He knows his life is limited with us," Cort said.

Becan continued to look up at her. "See for yourself. No barriers. I speak the truth. Dorran destroyed my blood brother's line."

"At least see what he has to show you," Jorn thought to her. *"Who knows what useful information we might learn."* He took the heart and sword from her.

She crouched in front of Becan to clasp one of his hands, her hand damp with blood. "Let me see."

Becan's gaze was fixed on her bloodstained hand. "Will you show me his death?"

"That depends on what you have to show me." She felt Jorn with her as she slipped inside Becan's memories. She saw Becan being held back while Dorran killed the young girl, saw him run to the body once he was set free, the child remaining in human form in death. Going further back in his thoughts she saw his brother holding a hunter in his arms, the woman skin and bone, demanding to know what was wrong with her. Shock arrowed through Morgane at the answer Becan's brother was given.

A hunter rested his hand on the woman's cheek. "You should never have bound your lives. A dragon and hunter don't belong together. Dragons are too selfish to share their power. They are only interested in taking all power for themselves. When she finally dies, so too will you. There's no way you can make it to the sacred waters in time to break the union. Not with the condition you're both in."

Morgane let go of Becan's hand as if struck, rising and stepping back. "He didn't make it in time?"

Jorn rested the sword against his leg and placed a

hand on her shoulder when Becan shook his head. *"You're different. You aren't the typical dragon."*

"What if I end up killing you? How do you know things won't change overnight? If a dragon that can fly can't make it to the sacred waters in time, what chance would we have?"

Becan continued to hold out his hand. "Will you show me Dorran's death?"

"If you let him go, how can you trust him to bring back another dragon?" Cort demanded.

She wanted to tell them all to stop talking. She might have been a Gold Dragon, but she was no warrior to lead others. Backing away, she shook her head. "I need to clean the blood off me before the sun sets and it becomes too cold to wash."

"I need to clean up too." Jorn followed her, carrying the heart and sword.

Hearing the other two start to follow, she spun to face them. "Light the fire or something. Catch something for dinner." Her gaze was drawn to Becan. "I'll be back before the sun sets. I'll show you then."

Becan nodded, giving Cort a menacing look when he started to protest.

She opened her mouth to tell them not to follow, closing it and striding away, words unspoken. How had she gone from no one in her life to a warrior wanting to swear fealty to her and two hunters temporarily at her side? She glanced at Jorn, who was physically at her side. "We'll visit the sacred waters as soon as we give the dragon bone to your village."

"I'm not at all weakened by you. The strength you shared with me has allowed me to do more than I'd normally have managed in a full seven days."

She doubted that would last. Even he'd said it'd take time for them to learn how to share their power equally. From what Becan had shown them, there'd be no sharing. The hunter who'd said dragons were interested in taking power for themselves had been right. She knew no dragon who'd share power if they could keep it all for themselves. And she was a dragon. The only dragon she'd ever been able to share power with was dead.

Taking the sword and heart from Jorn, she strode ahead to the river. Setting them on the bank, she removed her boots, belt pouch, bow and quiver. Laying her gear on the grass beside the other items, she entered the water. A shiver ran through her as she tried to stay warm.

Jorn set aside his weapons, boots and belt pouch before joining her in the river, drawing his shirt over his head to wash it in the flowing water.

She stared at his body, several faint scars along his

side. She looked up to see he watched her. "What are they from?"

"Last night wasn't my first encounter with russet cave bears. I was with a group of hunters, the previous time, and we lost three of them." He rung out his shirt, tossing it on the bank with the rest of the gear before ducking beneath the water.

She sank low enough to wash the blood from her shirt, the colour mingling with the water, gone before it could darken. Her gaze was again drawn to Jorn when he surfaced, half turned away from her. He ran his fingers through his hair. She couldn't stay bound to him, yet the thought of leaving him made her heart ache. When had he become important to her for himself and not because of his importance to Elin and Anja? And what was she going to tell Elin? That she'd let her brother bind their lives together to save her life and risk his own. How could she repay any of them like that?

Her gaze travelled along his back to where his body disappeared below the water. Was his skin as smooth as it looked? And those faint scars, did they feel different to the rest of his skin? What would it be like to be close to someone and not have to worry that Brigitte would kill them because of that closeness?

"I won't object."

"What are you talking about?" She met his gaze.

He looked over his shoulder at her, grinning. "Your overly admiring looks."

She felt her face warm, starting to turn away.

He was at her side impossibly fast, barely making a splash, his hands on her face as he cupped it, tilting her head up. "Take a closer look. The admiration goes both ways."

She stared into his eyes, her breath catching at the look she saw in them, remaining back from the emotions he invited her to examine. "I want more than admiration. I want something so strong you'd want to kill anyone who even thought about hurting me. That you'd rip out the heart of any who dared cross me and you'd claim me yours as I'd claim you mine. That you'd protect me above all others."

He didn't speak immediately. "I wish I could give you that. But I'd never lie to you or tell you I could think that way. I'd slay your enemies and I'd never want to cause you pain and I'd protect you from your enemies, but I can't imagine wanting to rip out the heart of someone."

"What if someone killed Elin?"

"I'd hunt them down and put an arrow through their heart. I wouldn't tear it from their body."

His words left her feeling hollow. "Then I guess I want a dragon, not a hunter." She wanted to comfort him when she saw the disappointment in his expression. She remained silent, holding herself still. It made sense. She was a dragon. Even with the bracelet that kept her from taking her true form. Even with Brigitte's insults about her being more hunter than dragon.

"When all this is over, we can make the journey to the sacred waters if that's what you desire. Not because you're worried about my health, but because you don't wish to endure this unity."

She inclined her head, having no idea what she desired. She didn't want to be alone, with only a warrior to serve her, but she didn't want to settle for something less than what she'd always dreamt of having. "What if it's too late by then?"

"Too late for what?"

For her to want to face the world alone? For her to let him go? She kept those thoughts hidden behind her many barriers, not sure they were enough to keep him out if he should look. "For your health. I care enough that I wouldn't want to be the cause of your death."

"How can you be the cause of something if another has chosen to make that decision?"

His hands were warm against her face, the water cold in comparison. She had no idea how to answer him. "The day is drawing to a close. I need to sort out what I should do next."

"What we should do." He leaned close, his lips a breath away from hers. "Did you really kiss Cort?"

"If you could call it a kiss."

"Show me?"

She wasn't sure if he meant physically or the images in her mind. It took her a moment to decide which one she wanted him to have meant. Leaning in, her lips lingered on his. She drew the moment out before putting space between them, her hands resting on his chest. "It was nothing like that." Smiling, she pulled away from him, wondering at what point his arms had encircled her, as she splashed through the water to the bank.

Jorn laughed, the sound filling the air as he came after her, reaching the bank at the same time as she did. "Good." He gathered his gear, putting everything back in place except his shirt which he carried, collecting the sword as well.

Once all her gear was in place, she picked up the heart, now gone cold, and followed him to the cave where she sat by the fire, trying to warm herself.

Cort stopped glaring at Becan long enough to

glance at the heart. "Are you going to carry that around until it begins to rot?"

"I need to decide what to do with it." She stared down at it, still uncertain.

"What are your choices?" Cort asked.

"Eat it all at once or save it to have over time."

Cort rose from where he sat by the fire, stumbling backwards in his haste. "You would eat your own people? Dragons are cannibals?"

"Dragons can't be judged by human standards." Becan gave Cort a disdainful look before turning to Morgane. "I could carry it to colder climates and find a place to store it for you if you wish to make it last. Or cut it up and use one of the various preserving methods."

Cort continued to back away. "Do you eat humans too?"

Becan looked him up and down. "What would be the point? There's nothing to gain from eating one of your kind."

"What do you gain from eating your own kind?" Cort demanded.

"A longer life." Jorn sat beside Morgane. "Sun is nearly down." He nodded to the colour in the sky.

Morgane held out a hand to Becan. "I'll show you

Dorran's death and if you wish to help me I'll accept your loyalty until my current task is completed."

Becan took her hand. His grip tightened as she showed him the death. Once it was done, he let go of her hand and knelt in front of her, pressing his arms and upper body against the ground. "That is the way a dragon should avenge a blood brother. My sword is yours for as long as you'll have it. In the morning, when I've recovered, let me bring you Dorran's right hand warrior to be taken to Cort's village. Let me weaken him as you weakened me."

Chapter Eighteen

Morgane touched Becan on the shoulder to let him know she accepted his offer before drawing out her dagger. Cutting two slices from the heart, she held one out to Becan.

Becan's expression was a mixture of shock and disbelief. "You'd give me a piece?"

She inclined her head.

"Why?"

Reasons filled her head. Easily half a dozen. Most she didn't want to speak. "Because you were prevented from taking the revenge you were entitled to. He should have been as loyal to you as you were to him."

Becan took the slice from her. "My life is yours. I am yours. Always."

"Don't–"

Becan interrupted her. "It's done." He ate the piece of heart.

"Isn't this what you wanted?" Jorn thought to her. *"Your own people."*

She looked past Becan to Jorn, making sure only he could hear her thoughts. *"Not like this. How will he feel when his gratitude wears off?"*

"Who's to say it will," Jorn thought to her. *"Would you discard his loyalty like Dorran did?"*

A fierceness rushed through her, mixed with anger at Brigitte's betrayal of Gwynham. *"Never."*

"Where does this leave your promise to me?" Cort demanded.

Morgane waved Becan back when he made a threatening move towards Cort. "I always fulfil my promises." She thought of her brother's heart as she ate the slice of Dorran's she'd cut off. "Always." Somehow she'd find Gwynham's heart once she'd made sure Elin and Anja were safe. She turned to Becan, wanting to offer him reassurances even though none were expected. "I accept your loyalty and appreciate knowing your sword is at my side. I'll do my best to never let you regret giving your loyalty to me."

Becan nodded towards the heart. "In the morning,

do you want me to fly it into the mountains where the snow remains on the ground year round?"

She removed the dragon-leather scarf from around her hair and wrapped the heart, giving it to Becan. "Yes. Show me the directions when you return."

Becan took the heart. "Is there anything you wish for me to do now?"

Jorn rose to his feet, spreading his shirt out by the fire. "Cort and I will scout the area."

"I want to know when I get a dragon to take back to my village." Cort remained seated.

Jorn grabbed him by the upper arm, dragging him to his feet. "When it's time. Now help me scout the area."

Cort looked over his shoulder as Jorn tugged him into the forest. "I've been told you should never trust a dragon."

"That's actually good advice." Morgane rose to her feet, managing not to look at Dorran's corpse.

Cort pulled away from Jorn to face her properly. "Does that mean I shouldn't trust you?"

A smile briefly appeared. It had been Gilda who'd first told her the saying. "You can take a dragon at their word, but never trust one where no bond is given."

"I can trust your word?" Cort asked.

She was tempted to read his mind at the hint of uncertainty she heard in his tone. "You can trust all dragons' promises, just make sure you understand exactly what they've said and the many nuances to what it might mean."

"Are you trying to tell me something about our deal?" Cort demanded.

"She's teaching you how to protect yourself from all dragons. If you're going to keep roaming this part of the forest you're going to need to know how best to do that." Jorn tugged Cort into the forest. "You can have this conversation later. We need to scout the area and make sure it's safe."

"He seems younger than his years," Becan said. "Do humans tend to keep their young weak?"

Morgane thought about how Brigitte blamed her inexperience on falling for the man who'd fathered her and Gwynham. "He's had too many protect him."

"Isn't that what you're trying to do?"

"Not exactly." Maybe Elin's habit of taking in injured animals had worn off on her. She smiled, doubting Cort would appreciate that comparison. "We need to remove all the bone and destroy the rest." She nodded towards the body.

They worked silently together, the task quicker with two. The bones were scraped of meat and stacked in the back of the cave, in yet one more pile, by the time the hunters returned. They were rapidly running out of space. They'd also scraped some bone from the bones of the common warrior in preparation for weakening more dragons. As well, Morgane had cleaned out her belt pouch and restocked the dragon bone she kept in it. The paste one and the one for her to consume.

Jorn and Cort brought back several rabbits. While they cooked, Cort asked about the experiments she planned to do.

Morgane glanced at Becan. "I already know the answers to my questions." She'd learned it in her fight with Dorran and from the comments Becan had made. Bone from a Gold wasn't needed.

"Then why did we need to bring him here?" Cort asked. "Other than for me to take a live dragon to my village."

"Because I didn't have all the answers I needed when you brought him back here."

Jorn interrupted Cort, looking to Morgane. "When will we have the necessary ingredient for the village to weaken and attack the dragons?" He took several tree nuts from his belt pouch and held them out to Morgane.

"We'll be ready tomorrow." She looked at the nuts. "What are they?"

"To dye your hair. Grind them up and add water until you have a thick paste to put through your hair and over your eyebrows. In the morning wash it out and you'll look like one of us. It'll protect you from being recognised as a dragon." Jorn dropped the nuts into her hand. "Let me know if you need help." He held several nuts out to Becan. "You might want to do the same."

"Thank you." Morgane echoed Becan's words.

Jorn met her gaze. "Some things can be more important than ripping out someone's heart. Such as doing something that will prevent a situation from reaching that stage." He nodded towards the nuts she held.

A grin escaped and she placed the nuts in front of her. Gilda would have been horrified to hear someone compare a simple offer of nuts to something as monumental as ripping out another's heart. "Some hearts need to be ripped out. But this is good too."

They had an early night, mainly so Morgane could avoid Cort's frequent attempts at learning more information and reaching an agreement on how he'd get a dragon to take back to his village. Morgane put the stain in her hair and over her eyebrows before retiring, noticing Becan did the same. They took turns at keeping watch. The task was made easier by the amount of them available to take a turn. As the grey light of dawn filled the sky, Becan took flight, taking the heart with him, having already washed the paste from his now brown hair and eyebrows.

Jorn came to stand beside her. "Are you worried for him or worried for us?" He glanced at her. "And no, I'm not in your head. The emotions are spilling out all over me."

"Both. All. Will your village let me go once I give them the dragon bone?"

Jorn rested a hand on her shoulder. "I'll make sure of it."

Breakfast was the last of the rabbit and venison. Afterwards, Morgane washed the paste from her hair, the dark brown, wet strands draped over her hand. It was odd after a lifetime of fair hair. Rising from the bank, where she'd crouched to wash her hair, she caught sight of Jorn watching her. She started to raise her hand to her hair, stopping before she could touch it.

Jorn crossed the space between them. "You look beautiful no matter the colour of your hair."

She raised her chin. "Strength is more important than beauty."

Jorn laughed softly. "Then you have plenty of both." He nodded towards the cave. "Ready?"

She nodded, walking beside him to the cave where she gave him some ground up dragon bone, the white powder fine enough it could be mistaken for several different common items.

Jorn wrapped the dragon bone in a broad, supple leaf and slipped it into his belt pouch. "Are you ready to leave?"

She turned to Cort. "Are you sure you understand the danger of travelling with us?"

Cort's hand went to his dagger. "This is why I left home. You don't have to protect me. I was trained to be a hunter. I want the opportunity to use that training. And to prove to my family I'm capable of more than they believe I am."

She inclined her head. "We'll see what we can do." Striding ahead of the hunters, she slipped her hand into her belt pouch and had some of the dragon bone from Dorran. She'd had some upon rising and before washing her hair, but it'd be a long day and she was likely to need extra.

They reached the village without incident, several hunters surrounding them as they approached, becoming visible to show they had bows aimed at them, arrows drawn back. Jorn held up the dragon bone Morgane had given him, wrapped in the leaf. "Tarben is expecting us."

The rest of the journey was made in silence. Not that the earlier part had involved much talking. At least it hadn't been an ominous silence like this one. They were taken to a thatch hut, two hunters guarding the entrance, one hand on the hilt of a sheathed dagger, the other holding a bow.

Morgane met their glares, raising her head as she returned an equally fierce glare.

Jorn stepped close, his arm brushing hers. *"I won't let them harm you. I do have a voice in this village."*

"Will you when they learn what you did?" Could he really expect his people to be happy with him binding himself to her? Even if it'd only be for a short time.

"Unless they choose to send me from the village I'll always have a voice here."

A hunter stepped out of the hut, beckoning them to enter. His glare was more fierce than the hunters standing guard. Morgane followed Jorn inside, Cort behind her. She recognised him from the night she'd rescued Anja. He'd been the second hunter to speak. *"Who is the unhappy hunter?"*

"Tarben's brother, Mikkel." Jorn stopped in front of Tarben, holding out the dragon bone. "As promised."

Tarben took the parcel from him, opening it. "This will weaken them?"

"If you can get them to consume it," Jorn said. "Or absorb it through a wound."

Morgane kept her face expressionless. She should have told him not to mention that part.

"We mixed some with deer fat and made a paste for our arrows," Cort said.

She barely managed not to say something to Cort. Something that was likely to have been accompanied with a growl.

Tarben's gaze went to Cort. "Where are you from? And how did you end up with Jorn?"

"A village three day's travel from here," Cort said. "On the shores of the Great Lake."

Tarben inclined his head. "I visited there many years ago. You have the look of some of their hunters. Older siblings? Or parents and uncles."

Cort shrugged. "Could be either. I'm the youngest of fourteen and my parents have many siblings too. The region is full of game and the climate mild. Our families tend to be large."

"How did you come to be with them?" Tarben asked again.

"The dragon promised me one of her kind to take back to my village." Cort nodded towards Morgane.

Chapter Nineteen

Morgane glared at Cort. So she was 'the dragon' now he was talking to his people?

"Sorry," Cort thought to her. *"I don't know how to address you in front of them. Do you have a title I can use rather than be overly familiar and use your name?"*

Her annoyance faded, vanishing when Jorn moved close so his arm pressed against hers. *"No title."* She'd taken up the bow instead of continuing to use the sword so she couldn't even claim the title of warrior according to Brigitte. She thought of her brother's sword hidden in the back of the cave. It had been difficult to leave it behind.

Mikkel gestured towards the powdered bone Tarben held. "How are we meant to make them eat it? There must be forty or fifty dragons at the castle."

"Less." Morgane smiled at the memory of killing Dorran.

Mikkel glared at her. "Not enough to make a difference."

"It isn't up to the dragon to find us a way to make them eat this ingredient, Mikkel. We're hunters. We've learned to trap and kill many a beast over the years." Tarben wrapped up the parcel. "This will be no different."

Morgane's gaze was momentarily drawn to the dragon bone before returning to Tarben. "Our part is done? You're satisfied?"

"We need to see what the results are first," Tarben said. "Need to know this will work as you've said."

"I saw it work on two dragons," Cort said.

Mikkel glared at Cort. "We only have your word you're welcome in your village. You might have been ostracised for siding with dragons."

"I'd never betray my people." Cort's hand went to his dagger as he took a step towards Mikkel.

Jorn held a hand in front of Cort. "I brought you here as a guest."

"I wouldn't have known from the way I've been treated." Cort continued to glare at Mikkel.

"The three of you may remain in Jorn's hut while plans are put in place."

The hunters guarding the door stepped inside, as if

having waited for Tarben to speak those words. They gestured towards the exit.

"What exactly does that mean?" Morgane thought to Jorn as she followed him outside, Cort once again behind her.

"A polite way of telling us we're prisoners until the matter is fully resolved." Jorn led the way to his hut, a thatch building on the outskirts of the village.

Cort looked around when he entered. "You're one of the lowest ranking hunters?"

"Why would you ask that?" Morgane demanded.

Jorn placed a hand on her shoulder. "The higher the rank, the closer you are to the centre of the village."

"Are you low ranked?" Her gaze was drawn around the single room hut. A low bed was off to her left, blankets and furs piled upon it, a firepit was in the middle of the compacted dirt floor and a timber table, four stools and a set of shelves were to the right. Directly ahead, past the firepit, was a wooden trunk with metal hinges and handles. It was nothing like the castle she'd been raised in.

Jorn chuckled. "I was offered another hut, closer to the centre, but this one is better. It doesn't leak when the rains come and the winds don't find their way inside during the colder season."

"You will always remain here on the outskirts if you don't accept another one," Cort said.

Jorn shrugged. "I'm content."

Elin burst into the hut, throwing herself at her brother. "Why are hunters guarding your door?"

Jorn returned her hug before stepping back. "Have you considered they might be there for our protection?"

"I doubt it." Elin turned to Morgane, hugging her as enthusiastically as she'd hugged her brother. "We have to find a way for you to stay nearby. You can't go north. I won't let you."

Morgane tightened her arms around Elin. "I'll miss you." She tried to step away.

Elin clung to her. "I mean it. You can't leave."

"I need to." Morgane finally broke free from Elin.

"Then Anja and I are going with you," Elin stated.

"Elin-" Jorn began.

"No. We're going too." Elin glared at her brother, as if daring him to disagree.

Morgane stepped between them. "I need to do this alone. I promised my brother." She couldn't take any of them north with her. It was too dangerous and even she might not return. But first, she had to travel to the sacred waters with Jorn to break the binding.

Jorn joined Morgane, standing at her side. "Think

you can arrange food for us, Elin? I doubt they'll let us wander around the village."

"You're hungry?" Elin looked at each of them. "Why didn't you say? I'll be back shortly."

Elin hadn't long left when Anja entered. "They wouldn't let both of us come in here at the same time." She slowly shook her head. "As if the two of us together would somehow change things."

Morgane started to tell Anja that they couldn't use them as hostages against them if they didn't keep at least one of them away at all times. Before she could speak, Cort stepped forward and smiled at Anja.

He held out his hand. "I'm Cort."

"I have no magic," Anja blurted out.

Cort's smile didn't dim. He stepped closer so he could take her hand. "Many in my village don't. It isn't important to most people."

Anja stared at him, open-mouthed for a moment. "Isn't important?"

Cort shrugged, still holding out his hand. "Not really. It isn't as if it's something you have any control over. Not like feats of daring or battles of honour."

"Oh." Anja took his hand. "I'm Anja. Where are you from?"

While the two talked, Jorn drew Morgane aside.

"You might want to have more of the bone," he thought to her.

"But I don't-" She broke off when she saw the flushed look of his face. She didn't feel weak, but he obviously didn't look that good. She pressed a hand against his face. *"It's starting, isn't it?"* She should have known it wouldn't take long.

"Have some bone. That'll give us both energy."

She turned her back on Cort and Anja. *"The bone won't last forever."*

"We'll worry about that when you're getting low." Jorn positioned himself to shield her actions from the other two.

She'd no sooner had the dragon bone, and her hearing had sharpened, when she heard Elin arguing outside that she wanted to take food in to her brother. She shared the conversation with Jorn who nodded and went to the door, taking the food his sister had brought.

The hunters weren't impressed, making Anja leave too. The day dragged by, food delivered again when the sun set. Morgane spent a lot of the time stretched out on the bed, resting and listening in to the various conversations in the village, regularly having dragon bone to allow her to do so and to keep herself from stealing Jorn's energy.

At one stage Jorn stretched out beside her, his skin warm. He shifted her hand when she pressed it against his face.

"We go to the sacred waters and break this next. I won't kill you," Morgane thought to him.

"I have no plans to die."

"Good. Then it's settled."

"Afterwards, we'll go to the north and I'll help you track down your brother's heart."

"Why?"

"I've never been north before."

"Tell me the real reason." She leaned up on her elbow to look down at him.

Jorn smiled. *"It is a real reason. It doesn't have to be the only reason."*

Cort looked over at them, pausing in his pacing. "What are you talking about?"

"Going north," Jorn said.

"I want to go north." Cort crossed the hut to sit on the edge of the low bed. "When are we going?"

"You'll be busy taking a dragon back to your village." She didn't need the responsibility of two hunters. She'd have Becan with her. A dragon. Someone willing to tear the heart out of an enemy. Her gaze was drawn to Jorn. Someone not human or likely to die because he was with her.

Jorn reached up to brush his fingers along her cheek. "You're not going alone. Never again."

"I'll take Becan with me."

"You're not going alone," Jorn repeated.

"I don't need your pity." She pulled away from him to step off the end of the bed.

He joined her, his hands resting on her hips. "You've never had my pity and you never will." His gaze momentarily rested on her lips before returning to her eyes. He thought to her, *"Only my admiration."*

"What is that meant to mean? Your admiration."

"You chose to do what was right even though it'd cause you to be alone in the world."

Pain washed over her, anger threaded through it. *"He was my brother. My twin. Part of me. We were curled in the same egg together, fighting for space, but willing to share. Usually one eats the other before hatching. How could I stay with those who killed him, no matter who they were to me?"*

Cort crossed the space to stand beside them. "What's going on? What aren't you telling me?"

Morgane stepped away from them, turning her back on them. "I don't need-" She broke off when Becan contacted her.

"I visited the castle to capture the warrior you can give to Cort, instead of me. They're expecting an attack tonight.

The hunter who made a pact with Brigitte warned her.” Becan sent Morgane an image.

She held up a hand in answer to Jorn and Cort's demands about what was wrong. *“That's Tarben's brother.”*

“Who is Tarben?” Becan thought to her.

“The prime hunter.” There was no way anyone would listen to her. Mikkel was one of theirs. More than one of theirs. The brother of the one with the highest standing in the village.

“What do you want me to do? I have three warriors who are willing to join you. Ones who don't want to swear fealty to Brigitte now Dorran's dead. They'd be willing to help,” Becan offered.

“I have no land. No castle. What do I need with warriors?” Frowning, she turned away from Jorn and Cort when both stepped in front of her again.

“Then we take the castle. We take from Brigitte the equivalent of what she took from you. Her greatest treasure.”

A thrill of excitement raced through her and she tried to tamp it down. *“That's madness. Four warriors can't take a castle.”* Yet she wanted to. The desire to take it from Brigitte burned through her. This was the plan she'd been searching for.

Jorn captured her hand, preventing her from turning away again. "Is it good or bad? I can't read the emotion clearly. I could almost believe it's both."

Not wanting the hunters guarding the hut to hear, she brought Jorn and Cort into the conversation. *"It's a trap."*

"What is a trap?" Cort asked.

"Elin said she's going with them," Jorn thought to Morgane.

"Tonight? The attack?" Cort asked. *"Anja went with them too."*

Jorn grabbed Cort when he started for the door. *"They won't let us out. Or believe us."*

"You're going to let them be killed?" Cort shook Jorn's hand from his arm.

"No. We're going out the back of the hut." Jorn strode to the chest and moved it to the side, using his magic.

"What do you want me to do?" Becan asked.

"Collect Cort and he can make the two of you invisible while you fly overhead and see what's happening." Morgane eyed the small door that was revealed.

"I can do that." Cort gestured to the small door. *"What is that for?"*

"Accessing the firewood stacked along the back wall of the hut when it's raining." Jorn opened the door and

brought in firewood, handing it to Cort who stacked it along the wall. When the opening was clear, he looked up at Morgane. *"You don't have to come with us. If you leave they might think you're part of the trap."*

She raised her chin, looking directly at him. *"You think I'd desert Elin and Anja?"*

Jorn grinned. *"No, but I had to make the offer anyway."* His grin faded. *"It'll be worse for you."*

"I know. But I was never staying in this village anyway so it doesn't matter."

Jorn inclined his head before vanishing.

Chapter Twenty

Morgane sensed Jorn move through the opening, Cort vanishing and doing the same. She was barely halfway out the small door when Jorn's hand rested on her shoulder, bending the light around her. Closing the door, she rose to her feet. *"Where are you, Becan?"*

"Do you want me to gather help?" Becan showed her his location, giving her an image of the ground he flew above.

"I recognise that location from when I visited this area a week ago to see what the castle looked like." Cort moved away from Morgane and Jorn. *"There's a clearing between there and here. I'll meet you in the clearing."*

"Morgane?" Becan asked.

She held onto Jorn's hand as they strode silently through the outskirts of the village, slipping her other hand into her belt pouch. *"We'll see what's happening first. Don't be seen. If you are, there's no way you'll be able to return to the castle."*

"I have no need to return." Becan paused a moment. *"I've landed, where are you, Cort?"*

"Nearly there. I can't move as fast as a dragon. I'll become visible when I reach you. You won't miss seeing my light," Cort said.

"Will you be far enough from the village that none of them will see you?" Morgane asked.

"I wandered around this forest for days and no one spotted me," Cort said.

At his tone, she started to tell him not to be overconfident. She kept the words to herself. *"Let me know when you're above the castle and can see what's going on."*

"I will," Becan said.

"What plan do you have for us?" Jorn asked once it was only the two of them in the conversation.

"I don't know, but we need to get closer. We're too far from the castle to do anything." She broke into a run, Jorn easily keeping up with her. *"How do you feel?"*

"Keep up the dragon bone. I feel full of power." Jorn momentarily tightened his hand on hers. *"When we travel to the sacred waters, I can try and remove the*

bracelet. *Magic is stronger while in the sacred waters. It amplifies it.*"

"*That wouldn't hurt you?*"

"*They protect and enhance. If your bracelet can be removed by magic, then it can be removed while in the sacred waters.*"

She could fly again?

"*That's what you felt earlier. That elation. What were you thinking about? Or talking about. It can't have been Elin and Anja in danger.*"

"*Becan suggested capturing the castle.*"

Jorn laughed aloud. "*I should have known.*"

"*Quiet.*"

"*You've given me more than enough power to deaden the sound so it can't be heard beyond our space. Are you going to capture it?*"

She recounted the discussion as they continued to run, needing to have another piece of shaved dragon bone. When he didn't immediately comment after she'd finished telling him, she demanded. "*Well?*"

"*Do you need help?*"

"*What do you mean, 'do I need help'? You can't think it's a good idea. We'd probably die.*"

"*Morgane, good idea or not, it's what you desperately want to do. I felt it. That is your equivalent to ripping your* mother's heart out. I'd be surprised if you could physically rip it out."

"Taking the castle is a terrible idea."

"Of course it's a terrible idea. But my offer stands. Do you need help?"

She wanted to say yes, but allowing him to help might get him killed too. Then it hit her and she stumbled. He was willing to help her metaphorically rip someone's heart out and risk his life to do it. She glanced at him, wanting to delve into his mind and see exactly how he felt. There wasn't time. They had hunters to rescue.

"You haven't answered me." Jorn slowed as they approached the castle, everything quiet.

"Get through this first. We can worry about the rest later." She came to a stop in front of the castle. Nothing moved. "Can you keep me invisible when you're not in contact with me?"

"It'll take more power. Twice the amount."

She had more dragon bone. "Give me your dagger and keep me invisible." She drew Becan and Cort into the conversation. "What can you see?"

"We've flown over the castle a dozen times and haven't seen a thing. No warriors and no hunters," Cort said.

"Even the humans aren't moving around like they

would at this time of night. I'd swear the castle is full of ghosts," Becan said.

Morgane took the dagger from Jorn. *"Wait here."* She threw herself at the wall of the castle, driving the daggers between the stones, scrambling up to the battlements. Her dagger handled the treatment better than Jorn's that snapped, the broken section long enough to get her up the last section. She landed on the battlements, the light still bending around her. *"I owe you a new dagger."*

"I wouldn't mind one of those swords your people use," Jorn said.

"A sword would be nice," Cort said. *"And knowing how to use it."*

"I can ask Devona to raid the armoury," Becan offered.

"I can't accept any other warriors. I can barely protect myself," Morgane said.

"It'll be more protection than they'll have by the morning," Becan said. *"None of them are staying. They're going to use the commotion to leave."*

"Where are they going? How will they survive?" She knew Devona. The warrior had taught her about battle planning. Brigitte had put an end to it when she'd learned, demanding to know who'd ordered the teaching. When Devona had said Gilda, Morgane

had added that she'd told Gilda that Brigitte had ordered it and had her fetch Devona. The warrior had known it was a lie yet she'd remained silent. *"Who else wants to leave?"*

"Tathen and Starne."

She hadn't had much to do with them. They were brothers that seemed to keep mostly to themselves. How did the three of them think they could survive this world without help? They'd be killed on sight. None of the villagers liked dragons and the savages attacked anything that moved. Even each other at times. If they left now, Brigitte would never forgive them or accept them back. *"Where are they?"* She ran lightly along the battlements, seeing no one. Dragon, human or hunter.

"Raiding the kitchen. Do you want me to ask them to raid the armoury?" Becan asked.

"Where is everyone?" Morgane asked. *"The warriors and Brigitte's hunters."*

"There are a dozen hidden at the back where the hunters will enter. Hidden by Brigitte's hunters," Becan said. *"The rest are hiding amongst the outbuildings."*

"Did any of them have the food that would weaken them?" Morgane asked.

"None. They knew all the details of the plan."

"Where is Brigitte?" Morgane entered the castle, hurrying through it headed for downstairs.

"In her rooms with a handful of warriors, a couple of her hunters, some humans and Gilda."

Fear for Elin and Anja raced through her. *"Jorn, Cort, how do we find hunters when they're invisible?"* She had more dragon bone before running outside. No one attacked and she scanned the area, looking for telltale signs of hidden warriors.

"Run into them," Jorn thought to her.

"Set an area alight," Cort answered at the same time.

"Oil." Morgane ran to the outbuilding where the lamp oil was stored.

"What do I tell the dragons?" Becan asked.

"They can be mine to protect if they gather weapons from the armoury and be ready to swoop down and save hunters when I set the grounds on fire. The rest of you remain near the back of the castle." Morgane slipped inside the building, trying to see if anyone was in there. She had no idea what to do with one dragon warrior let alone four. She'd worry about it later. If she managed to survive the night. But if they helped her save Elin and Anja then she'd do whatever she could to protect them.

"How would the dragons see us coming?" Cort asked.

"*They soaked the ground with water around the rear entrance,*" Becan said. "*They also scattered dry leaves across the ground leading up to the rear exit to make it harder for the hunters to maintain their silence.*"

Spotting a barrel of oil, Morgane tipped it on its side, rolling it to the door where she needed to stand it up again to get it through. Again she laid it on its side, using her dagger to put several holes in the barrel. The oil leaked through the timber and she pushed it towards the rear exit before returning to the outbuilding for another barrel of oil.

The moment she got the second barrel of oil through the door, an arrow came towards her. She sidestepped rather than catch it or knock it aside. Let them think a hunter had got past them. Stabbing the barrel a few times, she was forced to dodge several more arrows before she could roll the barrel across the grounds. She had more of the dragon bone.

"*Everyone's in place,*" Becan thought to her.

Arrows flew towards her, a sword slashing the air in front of her. She backed away, unable to get anywhere near the oil barrels. "*Can someone set the oil alight?*"

"*Starne volunteered. He said to make sure you knew he was the first to offer,*" Becan informed her.

An arrow grazed her side and she breathed in

sharply, hiding inside one of the buildings. About to ask what was taking Starne so long, he streaked towards the ground, a burning branch held between his front claws. Dropping it, he headed skywards, avoiding the arrows that flew around him.

Hunters and warriors became visible throughout the castle grounds. Beyond the castle, arrows flew through the exit, several hunters becoming visible.

"What are they doing?" Morgane demanded. *"Why don't they retreat?"*

"Facing death head on is better than dying with an arrow in your back," Jorn thought to her.

"They're all going to die?" She headed for the exit, avoiding the flames, warriors and hunters.

"The experienced hunters would have brought ones that either can't bend the light or can't do so for long. They'll stop hiding them if they think they have the magic to escape. Enough hunters will live that the village will survive," Jorn explained.

She wasn't about to let that happen. Elin and Anja would be amongst the ones who weren't hidden. For all she knew, they were already visible. She could only see a small section of the area behind the castle through the exit. One of the hunters fell to the ground, several arrows piercing him at once. *"Becan, you and the warriors collect the hunters as they become visible. Tell them Jorn and Morgane have sent you. That Mikkel betrayed them. Drop them at the edge of the trees so they can escape.*" As she watched, a hunter was dragged into the air, becoming invisible. "*How long can you keep yourself hidden, Cort?*" She had more dragon bone before drawing her dagger as she approached one of Brigitte's hunters who was firing upon the hunters beyond the castle walls.

"*Not much longer. I'm using too much magic to keep my seat,*" Cort thought to her.

"*When you can no longer hide yourself, remain behind and let Becan gather hunters on his own. You tell the hunters to return to their village.*" Close enough to Brigitte's hunter, she grabbed at his bow, slashing across his throat when he turned in that direction. He dropped to the ground at her feet and she ran for safety as numerous arrows came for her. When a hand grabbed her, she started to slash out at it, stopping when she realised it was Jorn. She'd been so busy trying to focus on everything she'd stopped keeping track of where her people were.

"You're not having enough dragon bone." Jorn spoke the words aloud. "You need a lot more than you're eating." When Morgane glanced at a nearby hunter, he grinned. "No one outside of where we're standing can hear my words."

She helped herself to more dragon bone, speaking aloud like he'd done. "I'm sorry about your dagger. I hope it didn't have a special meaning to you."

"No. I bought it from someone at the last gathering."

"I always wished I could attend one. Elin and Anja made them sound fascinating." They were held once a year at the foot of the mountains that led to where the sacred waters were. Each time Elin and Anja had been allowed to attend she'd listened, fascinated by the tales of celebrations, the forming of alliances, the array of items available for trade, the many dalliances they'd stumbled upon and the relationships formed.

"Morgane!" Brigitte's words rang out from the top of the battlements, a hunter on either side, Gilda in front of her. "Give yourself up or I will kill her. I knew you'd be back. It's the only reason I didn't kill her for the fires she set." She drew the sword that hung at her side.

Morgane took a step towards the battlements.

Jorn dragged her back. "She'll kill you instead."

Chapter Twenty-One

"I can't let her-" Morgane broke off when Gilda wrenched free from Brigitte, throwing herself over the battlements. Shock held her still for a heartbeat. "No!" She pulled out of Jorn's grip, becoming visible. She raced through the grounds, leaping flames, arrows flying around her. None of them pierced her skin, all of them scattering in a gust of air. Bursting through the exit, she raced to where Gilda would have landed. She came to a stumbling halt as she reached the location, finding nothing. They'd taken her body already?

"She's safe," Becan thought to her. *"Look up."*

Morgane slowly raised her head. A dragon flew towards the trees, Gilda clutched in her claws. A midnight blue dragon, almost impossible to see against the star studded sky. Devona. She experienced a moment of light-headedness at the relief she felt.

"Thank her for me." She didn't know them well enough to add them to the conversation without accidentally adding others or leaving the conversation vulnerable to eavesdroppers. Such as Brigitte. *"What about the hunters? How many still need to be rescued?"*

"They're all within the treeline. Including Elin and Anja," Cort informed her.

Relief again washed over her and she was glad Jorn drew her close, wrapping an arm around her waist, the light bending around them. *"We saved most of them?"*

"Three were lost. The bodies recovered," Becan thought to her.

"Help them return to the village." Morgane started towards the treeline, helping herself to more dragon bone, Jorn remaining at her side.

"They refuse to leave until the two of you speak to Tarben," Cort said.

"Are they crazy? The dragons could go after them." Morgane looked over her shoulder, half expecting to see the skies filled with dragons. There were none.

"What should I tell him?" Cort asked.

Morgane was about to say she'd speak to Tarben back at the village when something in Cort's tone had her frowning. *"What's wrong, Cort?"*

"What's your answer?" Cort asked.

"Becan? What's going on?" Morgane demanded.

"No, Becan," Cort said.

"She deserves to know," Becan said.

Morgane pulled away from Jorn, breaking into a run, pinpointing Cort's location. This time Jorn managed to keep her invisible.

"She doesn't deserve this after helping them avoid a trap," Cort argued. *"She saved them. Where is their honour?"*

Morgane came to a stop when she entered the treeline and spotted Tarben with a dagger at Cort's throat, several hunters around him. She directed her thoughts to Jorn as she had yet more dragon bone. It looked like she was going to need it. *"Make me visible."* She moved closer to Tarben, stopping within arms reach of him. She was about to once more tell Jorn to make her visible, when he did, remaining at her side and also becoming visible. She glared at Tarben. "Would you threaten an innocent hunter over what your brother has caused?"

Mikkel appeared beside Tarben. "None of them deserve to live. Kill them now and be done with it. Look at the mess you've made by listening to a dragon."

Morgane heard Becan land in the clearing behind

her, hearing two others land with him, all of them striding through the trees. *"Who's keeping watch?"* she thought to Becan.

"Devona. Gilda is with her. We didn't think you'd want us to risk your servant amongst the hunters," Becan thought to her.

"Well?" Morgane demanded of Tarben. "Why do you have a dagger at his throat? Didn't I join you as requested?"

"Why bring three dragons with you?" Tarben kept the dagger at Cort's throat.

"They didn't like how many hunters you have around you," Morgane said. "They like even less that one of them is a traitor."

"Are you going to listen to this?" Mikkel reached for an arrow.

Jorn drew one unnaturally fast, aiming it at Mikkel. "I wouldn't if I were you."

Mikkel froze, hand halfway to his quiver. "Make bargains with dragons and next thing hunters think they should side with them. And become one with them."

"Is this true?" Tarben's gaze went to Jorn.

"It was a temporary measure that will soon be undone," Jorn said. "But it changes nothing. We have a traitor in our village and they were there a lot longer than a handful of days."

"I know what this is." Mikkel lowered his hand, turning to Tarben. "You're the one in league with dragons and you're getting them to point the finger at me so no one realises."

"Twenty warriors have taken to the sky and are headed for the village," Becan thought to Morgane. *"Devona wants to know what you'd like her to do."*

"Where is Elin and Anja?" Jorn demanded of Tarben.

Morgane didn't need to wait for Tarben's answer. With the amount of power running through her, she knew exactly where they were. "They're in the village. How many hunters have returned? Enough to fight twenty dragons?"

"What rubbish is this?" Mikkel demanded.

Several hunters lowered their bows, looking in the direction of the village. One stepped forward. "What if she's telling the truth? My children are unprotected. The majority of the hunters are here."

"Becan, tell Starne to take that hunter and for Tathen to grab one of the ones who made a move towards the village and fly them home. Get Devona to leave Gilda somewhere safe and come here to collect a hunter. You do the same.

Jorn, can you make them invisible long enough for them to grab the hunters and get out of here?"

The moment Devona landed behind him, Jorn lowered his bow and slid the arrow back in his quiver, turning to brush a hand across each of the dragons.

"What are you doing?" Mikkel demanded.

The four dragons went invisible, four hunters being grabbed and vanishing moments later. Mikkel didn't get the chance to draw an arrow. Jorn again had one aimed at him.

"I'll let Cort go if you return the hunters," Tarben said.

"Is that really what you think happened?" Morgane demanded. "That we grabbed them so you'd exchange Cort." She checked her energy levels, eyeing the distance between her and Tarben. She was a Gold Dragon, trained for years to be a warrior. It was past time she accepted that. And found a way to reconcile the part of her that wished to be a hunter with the part that knew she was a dragon. A moment of clarity struck her. Setting aside her sword had been about escaping Brigitte's rule. She'd liked using it as much as she enjoyed using a bow. There'd been no need to choose one over the other.

"Why else would you have taken them?" Tarben demanded.

Morgane's lips curved into a mirthless smile. No one was taking anyone from her. Not Tarben and not Brigitte. "I protect what's mine." She crossed the distance in a blur, wrenching Tarben's hand from near Cort's throat, pushing him towards Jorn. "Whether they're dragon or hunter. Or villagers you've left unprotected." She reached for Jorn and Cort's minds. *"Invisible. Now."* She stepped back from Tarben as the light bent around her. *"We need to return to the village."* She didn't wait for them to answer, running towards the village, helping herself to more dragon bone. She was beginning to think she hadn't brought enough.

"The hunters are in the village and the dragons are attacking. What do you want us to do?" Becan asked Morgane.

"Protect them. We're on our way." Morgane forced herself to run faster, cursing the bracelet that bound her in this form. As a dragon she could have been at the village in next to no time, fighting the dragons that were coming for Elin and Anja. *"Protect Elin and Anja first. They're my priority."*

"Most of them are gathering towards the back of the village. There seems to be some sort of fortification here with rocks and a timber palisade behind it," Becan said.

Morgane changed her direction, planning to come

into the village from an angle that would bring her closer to the palisade. *"If they die, I will want to rip out the hearts of all those who allowed it to happen."*

"My sister wouldn't want innocent blood spilled on her behalf," Jorn argued.

"If they let her die, then how innocent are they?" For a moment she hated sounding like Brigitte. But only for a moment. A fierce protective feeling washed through her. She'd already lost one of hers. She wasn't about to lose another. She consumed more dragon bone as she reached the village. *"Let them see me come, Jorn."* The light stopped bending around her and she drew her dagger, leaping for a dragon who remained in his draconic form, slicing at the fragile wings.

The dragon became human, causing her to tumble to the ground, drawing his sword to spin and attack her.

Jorn appeared in front of him, an arrow drawn back.

Before Jorn had the chance to release the arrow, Morgane was on her feet and plunging the dagger into the dragon's side. An arrow pierced his heart and the warrior became a dragon again, collapsing on the ground. She leapt over his body and attacked another dragon, this one flying in low to grab a villager who ran towards the palisade, landing on his back.

The dragon spiralled to unseat her.

She sank the dagger into his back behind his wings, wrapping her legs around him and clinging tightly. When he shot into the sky, she pulled out the dagger, stretching to slice into his wing. He leaned to the side, his wing working erratically. She sliced into it further and the dragon lost height. Leaning to the other side, she slashed at the other wing. The dragon sank closer to the ground and she leapt from his back onto another dragon that flew nearby.

Sliding across the scales, she stabbed the dagger in, halting her fall. It didn't help for long. He spun in midair and she hung from him for a heartbeat before the dagger pulled from his flesh. Arrows flew above her. The dragon swooped to dodge them and she grabbed hold of his leg, jerking herself to a halt. The dragon roared, spinning once more. She was tossed in the air, but managed to hold on, her energy ebbing slightly. When he righted, she let go of him to drop onto a dragon flying beneath her, her dagger catching on his wing and shredding through it as she slid towards the ground. She was too high above the ground to survive the fall and grabbed at a wing vein, momentarily slowing her descent. The dragon plummeted and she leapt from him before he hit the ground, coming up in a crouch.

Jorn stood across from her, firing arrows at the dragons flying overhead, aiming for the wings like she'd done. Around his feet were arrows sticking out of the ground, those he fired at the dragons curving back to plunge into the dirt.

Worried at all the magic he was using, she had more of the dragon bone as she turned to face a sound behind her. A dragon landed, changing into human form. She launched herself at him before he could draw his sword, her dagger driven up under his ribcage. Pulling it out, she drove her hand into the opening. Warm blood coated her hand. She wrenched the heart from his chest. He dropped to the ground, returning to his draconic form. She stood above him, dagger in one hand, heart in the other, her gaze fixed on the sky. The dragons flew towards the castle. She wanted to roar at the sky and raise her hand, that held the heart, high. But she was trapped in this form. Sheathing her dagger, she surveyed the village, satisfaction arrowing through her at the sight of the dead dragons.

"The hunters have arrived," Becan thought to her. He dropped down beside her, becoming human as he landed. *"We should leave. Even though we helped them, they want us dead."*

Jorn joined them, bow in his hand, arrows returned

to his quiver. "Go. I'll meet you at the cave." He drew her to him, holding her close as he stared into her eyes.

She remained pressed against him, her gaze roaming his face, relieved to see he was unharmed.

His lips met hers and his arm tightened around her. Drawing back slightly, he again met her gaze. "After we visit the north, we'll take the castle from her."

"Why?"

His lips curved into a smile. "Because winning suits you." Letting her go, he strode towards the hunters entering the village, balls of light held by some of them.

"Starne has Cort. I'll take you." Becan shifted into a dragon, waiting until she was on his back before he launched into the air.

Chapter Twenty-Two

Morgane mentally searched those below. Elin and Anja were safe. Her gaze was drawn to the bodies scattered across the ground. Four dragons and two villagers. She reached for Jorn's mind. *"Have them burn the dragons. Away from the village so you don't have to worry if they decide to come after the bodies."*

"I will. And keep your energy up. I have no idea the distance at which energy will continue to be drawn when it comes to hunter and dragon bindings."

She smiled at his order. As if she'd do anything else. She had some of the dragon bone, enjoying the wind blowing into her face. She missed being able to fly. Her fingers brushed across the bracelet. Soon. They'd travel north to the sacred waters and undo that which would cost Jorn his life and remove the bracelet. Then, once she'd found Gwynham's heart, she'd go after the castle and drive Brigitte from it.

Brigitte should never have killed Gwynham. She'd make sure she well and truly regretted that decision.

Becan landed in front of the cave, the other dragons already there. He waited until she was on the ground before he became human. "The weapons were collected from where they were stashed during the fights and have been put inside the cave. Gilda is in there too. Sleeping."

"She's unharmed?" Morgane took a step towards the cave.

"Exhausted, but unharmed." Becan gestured the other three dragons forward. "They wish to offer their fealty."

The three dragons knelt in front of Morgane, arms and bodies pressed against the ground, each repeating that they offered their fealty to her. Devona offered hers for a year with the option to increase the term later and the other two offered theirs until Brigitte was dead.

"And if she doesn't die?" Morgane asked.

Starne shrugged. "A dragon on their own has no chance of survival. Anyone is preferable to her. And you're far better than what we could have hoped for. We saw how fiercely you fought for those you've claimed. Even in human form you're more warrior than most."

Morgane inclined her head. "I accept those terms." She turned to Devona. "Thank you for saving Gilda." She held out the heart she'd taken. "It isn't Gold, but it's the heart of my enemy. One that went against mine."

Devona took it. "Thank you."

Morgane inclined her head once more before turning to Cort who watched in fascination. "I'll see that you have your dragon before I go north."

"Who needs a dragon. What we did at the village was amazing. A small group of hunters and a handful of dragons held off twenty dragons. We managed to kill some of them. That's a story that will be talked about for generations to come and I was one of the hunters." Cort's eyes were alight with excitement. "I'm coming north with you. If legends are told of your encounter with the creatures of nightmares, I want to be a part of them."

"They're wyverns," Becan said.

Cort frowned. "What do you mean?"

"The creatures of nightmares. They're wyverns. Vicious beasts who are the natural enemy of dragons and would take out a human in a heartbeat." Becan showed them an image in their minds. A winged creature with a barbed tail, long claws and clawed wings. "Several nests of wyverns."

Tathen drew close. "Wyverns." He grinned. "They can't resist gathering a hoard filled with valuable jewels and gold. When are we going north?"

"We need to wait for Jorn to return." She mentally searched for him, unable to find him at this distance. Her fingers brushed across her belt pouch. She'd have some soon. When no one was watching her. "I need a wash. Someone can build up the campfire." She waved Becan away when he would have followed her.

Once she'd washed and had some dragon bone she returned to the cave, changing out of her wet clothes and into the spare set she'd brought with her. She sat by the fire, her gaze caught by the sword leaning against the entrance wall. "My sword. Who collected it?"

"Devona. Gilda told her where it was," Becan said.

Morgane glanced at Gilda who was asleep towards the back of the cave, wrapped in the cloak she'd left behind. "I need a scabbard for my brother's sword." She glanced around the cave, frowning. "Where's Cort and Tathen?"

Starne shared a look with Becan before answering. "Gathering things."

Her gaze narrowed. "What things? And where are they gathering them from?"

Starne raised his chin. "You set no first warrior to give orders in your absence."

Devona strode inside. "I said this place wasn't fit for you to stay in. You're reduced to sleeping on the ground. Tathen said if he had a hunter who could keep him invisible he could sneak in and at least gather bedding for you to sleep on."

She looked at each of them, trying not to panic at the thought of Cort at the castle. He'd already used a lot of magic. What was he thinking? Legends weren't told about the ones who lost. She tried to tell herself she shouldn't be worried about a hunter. There were more than enough she needed to take care of without worrying about him. But somehow he'd become one of hers too. She faced Becan, making sure only he could hear her thoughts. *"What was your suggestion?"*

"That we don't want to be weighed down with unnecessary items on our journey north."

She drew away from him, asking the same question of Starne and Devona. The first shrugged and said there was no reason they shouldn't go if they wanted and Devona pointed out that someone had to make sure she was provided with necessary items. Morgane was tempted to point out she wasn't Brigitte and had different priorities. They didn't include risking the lives of her people for a handful of blankets. She turned back to Becan, speaking aloud. "You're my first warrior. Inform the others when they return. I'm going to sleep. Starne, you return to the area around the castle in case your brother needs help and check on Jorn for me." She retreated to the back of the cave, lying next to Gilda, wishing she had her cloak. The ground was cold. She moved closer to Gilda, the warmth not enough to keep out the cold. It took her a moment to realise she needed more dragon bone. Having several pieces, she closed her eyes, trying to sleep. Images filled her mind. Ones of the fights, finishing with the one of her holding the heart of her enemy. A fierce feeling again washed through her. They'd take the castle. Take from Brigitte her greatest treasure, just like she'd taken Gwynham, her greatest treasure. An ally who'd stood by her since before birth.

The grey light of dawn was filtering into the cave when Morgane was woken by Jorn draping a blanket over her. She drew him down beside her, keeping hold of his hand that was hot to the touch. "You're unwell." She slipped her other hand into the belt pouch, glancing around to make sure none watched her have some dragon bone.

"It was a long night." He stretched out beside her.

She mentally searched for Cort, finding him by the

fire. She wished she could take blood from the rest so she could keep track of them, but doubted they'd willingly let her have any. "What did Tarben say?"

Jorn drew her close. "You're cold."

"I'm accustomed to a higher body temperature." The warmth of him sank into her and she pressed herself against him. "Tarben?"

"He doesn't believe his brother would go against them. There are those who've said it's possible since Mikkel has been away more than usual and with no game to show when he returns. But he argued that any can return without game. It happens at times."

"Will Elin and Anja be safe there?"

"As much as anyone will be safe remaining in the village while Brigitte is nearby."

"Is that why you're going to help me take the castle?"

He laughed softly. "Try again." He paused a moment, his laughter fading. "Why is it so much easier for you to believe I'd do this for someone else?"

She tried to think of how to explain, deciding that each explanation sounded worse than the previous. "Sleep. We need to travel to the sacred waters when we wake."

He wrapped his arms around her. "It won't change anything." He closed his eyes.

She wanted to disagree. Of course it'd change things. He'd no longer be tied to her and could return to his life. She frowned. It shouldn't bother her. She wanted a dragon, not a hunter, in her life.

Jorn's arms momentarily tightened around her as he opened his eyes. "Stop thinking and go to sleep. How can you expect me to sleep when your emotions keep tugging at me?"

She opened her mouth to argue, closing it, her words unspoken. It was a little impossible to deny something she was finding difficult to hide from him. "The sooner we go north, the better." She closed her eyes on his smile, not at all tempted to return it. Well, not much anyway.

The next time she woke, it was to a whispered argument by the fire. She pulled out of Jorn's arms to sit up, frowning at Devona and Cort. The warrior needed to learn this wasn't the world her ancestors had come from. It was different here. "Let him eat. No one needs to wait until I've eaten." She might be a Gold, but she wasn't exactly a warrior. At least not the type of warrior a dragon was expected to be. She reached for her bow and quiver as she rose to her feet. She'd chosen to focus more on the skills of a hunter. But that would change.

Becan brought two swords to her, both sheathed. "Which one do you wish to use?"

For a moment she stared at Becan, wondering if he'd overheard her thoughts. Checking, she was reassured that no one would have heard. Her gaze was drawn to the swords. They were almost identical and had been made for her and Gwynham. She sensed Jorn move close, the unnatural heat radiating from his body when he drew near. Her hand hovered over Gwynham's sword for a moment before taking her own. She nodded to her brother's sword. "Give it to Jorn. And a dagger if anyone collected one."

"Several daggers were taken," Becan said.

Cort looked up from the food he was eating. "Do I get a sword too?"

Morgane turned to Becan, a question in her gaze. When he nodded she glanced at Cort before returning her gaze to Becan. "See to it."

Becan handed the sword to Jorn. "I'll choose a suitable sword for Cort and a dagger for Jorn."

"Thank you." Morgane headed outside, having dragon bone once she was out of view. Her body warmed a little and she tried not to think about how cold it would be heading north. As a dragon, it wouldn't have bothered her. Bound to her human form it would be difficult if she didn't manage to remove the bracelet.

Returning to the cave, Morgane ate the food Devona handed to her, nodding when the warrior mentioned there were warmer clothes in the cave and plenty of blankets if they planned to be gone a few days. Morgane watched Gilda who busied herself at the fire, checking the food that was cooking. "I need someone to stay here and protect Gilda."

Gilda looked up from the fire. "You'll need all your warriors. You've never faced wyverns before. If they're the same as the ones found in our world, they're vicious creatures that are difficult to kill."

Finished eating, Morgane rose to her feet. "Someone will remain with you." She met Gilda's gaze. "And this is my world. It's where I was born."

Gilda shook her head, opening her mouth to speak.

"I'll stay," Devona offered before Gilda had the chance to say anything. "I can scout the area and start planning what we need to do to take the castle." She nodded to Cort and Jorn. "A pity we don't have more hunters. Taking the castle by stealth would be the perfect method."

Jorn took the cloak Becan handed him. "There's no hunter I'd trust not to attack Morgane instead."

"What about your sister?" Cort asked.

"No. She isn't skilled enough at magic. She wouldn't be able to hide both herself and a dragon."

"Being able to hide herself would be useful," Devona said.

Becan continued to hand out cloaks, glancing at Morgane before returning his attention to Devona. "Plan with what we currently have. A small force can take a castle if it's done right. Especially since most of the humans don't care either way who holds the castle and Brigitte hasn't the warriors needed to fight off repeated attacks. We could harry them until there are only enough left for us to face."

Morgane slipped the cloak around her shoulders. "We have other things to worry about for now." She strode outside, glancing over her shoulder. "Time to leave."

They all traipsed outside, the three dragons shapeshifting so Morgane and the hunters could clamber onto their backs. Morgane lightly touched on each of their minds, making sure she knew them and would be able to add them to any conversation without worrying about letting others eavesdrop or adding the wrong person.

They headed north, Morgane grateful for the cloak she drew around her, having some dragon bone when she looked at Jorn and saw his drawn appearance. It was a good thing dragons were fast. She doubted he'd last another day.

Chapter Twenty-Three

It was well before the middle of the day when they saw the encampment set up at the base of the mountains. They circled the area, flying over the cave entrance to the sacred waters.

"How will we know if someone is in there?" Morgane directly asked Jorn.

"By entering."

That was what she'd feared. She sent her next thoughts to all of them. *"Land well away from the entrance, but in sight of it. No attacking the hunters in the area."*

"What if they attack us?" Starne asked.

"Avoid them." Morgane clambered off Becan's back once she'd had more dragon bone. *"Starne, return aloft and keep watch. Tathen, you stay on the ground and watch the entrance."*

Cort glanced around the area, speaking aloud. "I can't believe we're here already. It takes nearly a week to get here from my village."

"Two to three days for us, depending on who is travelling with us," Jorn said.

Cort stared at Tathen. "How long would it take you to see the entire world?"

Tathen shrugged. "Never tried."

"Now that'd be something worth finding out about. Who knows what undiscovered things might be in our world."

"The rest of the world will have to wait." Morgane held out her hand to Jorn. *"We have other things to deal with."* She continued to speak in their minds, not knowing who might be nearby, wishing that everyone else had done the same. She couldn't hear or smell anyone, but that didn't always mean anything. If a hunter had remained still in an area for some time, the creatures would have returned. And if the hunter was hidden, she wouldn't be able to smell or hear them.

"What is the plan?" Becan asked.

"Cort, keep you and Becan invisible. We'll see if anyone is at the sacred waters." As Morgane gave her orders, the light bent around her and Jorn and she smiled at him. Her smile faded when she saw how terrible he

looked. "Jor-" She started to speak aloud, not wanting to share her concerns with the others.

He pressed a finger against her lips. "We're nearly there. Stop worrying."

She nodded, striding towards the cave entrance as she had more dragon bone. *"Time to go inside."* She sent the thought to all of them.

The cave wasn't as dark as she thought it might be since her ability to see in low light was impaired. Glowing liquid ran down the walls, the interior of the cave warm and humid. They continued further in, no sounds greeting them.

Stepping into a larger cavern, Morgane stopped, her mouth open as she stared at the pool of water in front of her, the four of them becoming visible. The water glowed with the same bluish white as the water that ran down the walls, mist rising from it. "What is it?" She spoke the words aloud, her hushed tone sounding hollow in the cavern.

"The sacred waters," Cort said.

"No." She shook her head, her gaze focused on the water that cast an eerie light on them. "The water. What is it?"

"Pure magic," Jorn said.

Becan stood at Morgane's shoulder. "Magic? How is that possible?"

Jorn shrugged, tugging on Morgane's hand. "Do you want me to try and remove the bracelet?"

She hesitantly followed him. "Should you separate us first?"

"It'll be easier to do the bracelet first." Jorn stopped by the edge of the water, removing everything except his trousers.

Cort joined them. "Do you want me to help? Two hunters should be stronger than one."

Morgane looked from one to the other, her gaze eventually resting on Cort. "Why would you help me?"

"You're not what I thought you'd be." He chuckled. "Not at all like I thought you'd be."

"That doesn't really answer my question."

Cort frowned, glancing at Jorn, before returning his attention to Morgane. "You really don't understand."

Jorn took her hand in both of his. "Friends don't need a reason. They'll help when you need them to."

Morgane met Jorn's gaze, looking into the depths of his brown eyes, trying to figure out what she saw in them. "You're my friend?"

"Cort is."

She glanced at Cort before speaking to Jorn. "Then what are you?"

He didn't answer immediately. "Sadly, not what you're looking for."

She wanted to apologise. Or comfort him. His words sent a wave of confusion through her. She decided to focus on what she could deal with and turned to Cort. "If you think having the two of you focus on opening the bracelet will work better, then I'd appreciate your help."

Cort began to remove his gear. "It can't hurt."

"What do you want me to do?" Becan asked.

Morgane tugged her hand from Jorn's grip, removing everything but her trousers and shirt. "Keep watch." Taking a deep breath, she stepped into the water, expecting it to be cold. The warmth seeped into her body, curling through it.

Jorn chuckled, joining her in the water. "The warmth of it surprises you?"

"Water is usually cold." She followed him further from the edge, the water rising until it reached her shoulders.

Cort joined them. "It's been a few years since I was here."

"When you turned eighteen?" Jorn asked, taking Morgane's hand.

Cort nodded, reaching for both Morgane and Jorn's hands.

She stared at the flickering light that crackled through the water. "Is it supposed to do that?"

"Yes," Jorn and Cort said at the same time.

"It recognises the magic in us and between us," Jorn said.

"This should work." Cort let go of her hand and the flickers of light stopped. He pressed a hand against her bracelet.

Jorn did the same, also letting go of Cort's hand to clamp his hand over Cort's that was on the bracelet. Cort did the same with his other hand.

Morgane felt the warmth increase in the metal, the flickers of light becoming forked streaks, like lightning branching out through the glowing waters. She felt all the hair on her body rise. The heat in the metal and water increased. Opening her mouth to ask what was happening, pain slashed through her and she screamed instead, the sound echoed by Jorn and Cort, light crackling around them.

"Morgane." Becan jumped into the water, forcing his way through it, his hands wrapping around Jorn and Cort's wrists.

A flash of light filled Morgane's mind and everything went dark. She woke to find Starne peering down at her, the rough, damp rock of the cavern beneath her back. "What happened?" She struggled to sit up.

Starne helped her. "Whatever it was, it felt like our minds exploded. Tathen felt it too. We came running in here to find the lot of you at the bottom of the water. Pulled you out, expecting you to be dead."

Spotting Jorn lying beside her, she crawled over to him, pressing a hand against his heart. It beat strongly. She stared at the bracelet that remained on her wrist. "It didn't work."

Groaning, Cort sat up. "What happened? Why do I feel so odd?"

"What do you mean–" Morgane broke off as she realised. "No." She stumbled to her feet, brushing away Starne's help. "No. We need to fix this."

Cort staggered after her, grabbing her arm before she could enter the water. "Not today. You can't go in again today."

Morgane pulled out of his grip. "This wasn't meant to happen. We were meant to fix things, not make them worse."

"What do you mean make them worse?" Cort asked.

Morgane's gaze was drawn to each of them. Cort, Jorn and Becan. "All of you. I can sense all of you. The same as I can sense Jorn."

Cort frowned. "What do you mean?"

She indicated all of them with a circling motion of her hand. "Joined. Together. Like we are bound to each other."

Cort stumbled back, shaking his head halfway through her explanation. "That can't be possible. We didn't-" he broke off. "This is wrong. You can only bind yourself to one other. This isn't possible." He backed further away.

"Then why do I feel you both in the same way I feel Jorn?" Morgane demanded.

Groaning, Becan struggled to sit up. "What happened?" He rubbed at his forehead. "What are you two doing in here?" He looked from Starne to Tathen. "Get out there and keep watch." He waited until the two of them had headed for the exit before he spoke to Morgane. "Why aren't you blocking? If there are dragons in the area, they'll hear you." He frowned. "They'll hear all of you." He rose to his feet, catching himself when he staggered. "What happened to us?"

Morgane had no idea what to tell him. It was almost a relief when Jorn rolled silently onto his side and pushed himself up off the ground, preventing her from answering Becan. That was until he spoke.

"Did it work?"

She couldn't answer him. Didn't want to answer him. It had been so far from working, that somehow they'd ended up doing what was probably the opposite.

"Why can I-" Jorn broke off to look at Cort and Becan. "Us?"

Cort was the only one who answered. He nodded.

"But-" Jorn shook his head. "This isn't possible." He closed his eyes. "Look at the ground in front of my feet, Cort." The moment Cort did, Jorn walked steadily towards him. He opened his eyes when he was an arm's length away from Cort. He stared silently at the other hunter for a moment. "This should not be possible."

"It's true?" Morgane asked. "The four of us?"

Jorn continued to stare at Cort, nodding.

"How do you know? This has to be a mistake," Morgane said.

Jorn faced her. "Because I was able to see through his eyes. Like we were one. Like hunting companions. Bound. But this shouldn't be possible. You can only bind yourself to a single person. The magic doesn't allow anything else."

Becan studied Jorn. "This could be useful. What other abilities does this give us?"

Morgane spoke before Cort or Jorn had the chance.

"We can't keep things like this. Us." She looked from Jorn to Cort and back again. "It will kill you."

"Kill us?" Cort asked. "Becoming any kind of partner through the use of magic doesn't kill."

"Unless one of those partners is a dragon." Morgane's gaze was drawn to Becan. "I can't imagine how much worse it must be when there are two dragons."

"There's a procession headed towards the cave entrance," Starne thought to them.

Morgane began to gather her gear. "When can we return to fix this?"

"It's too late. We didn't know hunters had gone ahead of the procession. They just became visible at the entrance to the cave," Starne warned.

Jorn pulled on his shirt, buckling on his belt. "We'll hide off to the side. We'll stay invisible until they're distracted then sneak out."

Finished putting on all her gear, Morgane looked around the area for somewhere to wait. "How long will they remain in here?"

Jorn shrugged. "Hard to say."

Cort finished putting his gear back on. "Depends on what they're coming here for." He grabbed hold of Becan's hand, the two of them disappearing.

Jorn moved close to Morgane. "I'm sorry we

couldn't remove the bracelet." Taking her hand, he bent the light around them.

"We need to return. What will being bound to two dragons do to you and Cort?" She moved silently to the side of the cavern with him.

"It feels different," Jorn said. "Not only because there are four of us bound together. I almost feel like I could fly."

She frowned. "I feel like something is crackling under my skin."

"That's what magic feels like. Energy running beneath your skin, waiting for you to use it. And the longer you go without using it, the stronger the sensation becomes."

Her grip tightened on him. "What happened to us?"

He met her gaze, his words soft. "I don't know."

"Can we fix it?"

He didn't answer, holding her gaze a moment longer before looking in the direction of the entrance where movement caught their attention.

Chapter Twenty-Four

Morgane watched several hunters and three villagers enter the cavern. The villagers were dressed in very little, the two males in trousers and the female in a shift. The hunters with them wore their usual clothes and carried their typical weapons. "What are they doing?"

"Those three will be eighteen. They'll take turns entering the sacred waters to see if their magic is strong enough for them to become hunters." Jorn moved slowly towards the exit.

Morgane sensed Cort and Becan do the same. *"Are the guards still at the entrance?"* She directed her thoughts to Starne and Tathen, including them in the conversation too.

"They haven't moved," Starne said.

"There should be enough space for you to pass between them if you go single file," Tathen said.

"*We'll go first and test it can be done,*" Becan said.

Morgane sensed them approach the exit. "*Don't risk it if you think it's too dangerous. We can remain in here until they leave.*"

"*I can't keep us hidden that long,*" Cort said.

Jorn glanced at Morgane's belt pouch, speaking aloud. "Do you think it would work?"

"I don't know." She also spoke aloud, not sure if she should share the information with Cort. Becan she could trust due to the oath he'd made to her.

"Try. We need to know how having another two changes things." Jorn tugged her to a stop, remaining against the cavern wall, the tunnel nearby.

She met his gaze for a moment, trying to figure out what to do. She didn't understand hunters. Not as well as she understood dragons.

Jorn smiled, brushing wet strands of her hair back from her face. "Cort would be as bound to keep your secrets as I am. But as a friend, he wouldn't think of telling another something that might harm you. Or cause problems for you."

Morgane slipped her fingers inside the belt pouch, taking out some bone shavings. "Do you feel weak? Or unwell?"

"No. I've never felt so healthy and fit in my life.

But that doesn't mean we should leave it till we're desperate to find out how things have changed."

"We've reached the exit," Becan said. *"If we're spotted, we'll draw them away to give you a chance to escape."*

"Hold on a moment," Cort exclaimed. *"They'll attack us."*

"Then we might as well make it count," Becan said.

She didn't like the idea of either of them being used as bait for her to escape. *"If you're spotted, flee. I will not have either of you injured on my behalf."* She brought dragon bone to her lips. *"Wait a moment. Tell me if this changes anything."* Eating the bone, she felt a rush of energy fill her. The crackle beneath her skin became more pronounced.

Jorn grinned down at her. "Seems to work even better now."

"How did you do that?" Cort asked. *"And how often can you do it? I wonder if this is what it feels like to be a prime hunter."*

"How did you do it?" Becan asked.

"I'll tell you later. When we get out of here," Morgane said.

"Move closer to the exit," Becan said. *"Be ready to run if they should notice us."*

She hurried forward, Jorn keeping close to her. *"I meant it when I said I want you to flee if you're spotted."*

"I'm your first warrior," Becan stated.

"What does that mean?" Cort asked.

"That I will always put myself between Morgane and danger," Becan said.

She wanted to protest. She didn't need anyone to put themselves between her and danger. She was more than capable of facing danger. But she knew he wouldn't listen. All she could do was make sure she was close enough to help if they were spotted. She sensed the two of them directly ahead of her. *"Go. I'm ready."* She kept to herself that she was ready to protect them, not escape.

Jorn laughed softly, speaking aloud. "If he knew you as well as I do, he wouldn't be continuing past those guards. He'd be arguing about your intentions."

For a moment she feared she'd not kept her intentions to herself.

"Don't worry." Jorn grinned at her again. "They don't know what you're thinking."

Morgane moved closer, her gaze fixed on the guards, her senses following Becan and Cort's movements. Her hand rested on the hilt of her sword when both guards faced the gap between them. One of them frowned. Morgane started to draw her sword. She wasn't about to let them harm any of her people.

Jorn rested his hand on hers, preventing her from drawing the sword. "Not yet. Give them a chance."

She left her sword sheathed, remaining ready to protect if necessary. She sensed Cort and Becan move past the guards, but didn't relax. They weren't safe yet.

The guard on the left stepped closer to the other one. "Did you sense that?"

Morgane remained where she was. Neither of them would be able to get past the guards.

The second guard shrugged. "I don't know. It was like magic in the air. That sensation of when you leave the sacred waters."

"Maybe you shouldn't have had the dragon bone," Jorn said aloud. "My magic feels so strong at the moment it's like my skin can barely contain it."

"What do you want me to do?" Becan asked.

Morgane eyed the two guards, looking back at the tunnel they'd travelled along. *"I say we give him the magic he was asking about."* She couldn't prevent a smile from forming. Didn't want to.

"What is the plan?" Becan asked.

"You two go further away from the exit. And make sure you're not directly in front of the opening." She tugged

Jorn close to the wall of the tunnel. *"Make it seem like magic is coming along the tunnel towards them. In a rush of air or something. Use it to force them aside so we can step past without them knowing we're here."*

Jorn nodded. A roar of air headed along the tunnel towards the exit. It rushed past the guards, knocking them aside. He dragged her out of the tunnel with him, hurrying past the guards who were picking themselves up off the ground.

"How did you do that?" Cort asked. *"I've never seen anything like it before. Small gusts, but nothing that strong. Do you think I'll be able to do it?"*

Morgane had no idea and guessed Jorn didn't either since he didn't answer Cort's question. She glanced frequently over her shoulder, watching the confused guards try and figure out what had happened. From what they were saying, it was nothing they'd ever encountered before. More power and more force than any of them had ever heard of when it came to magic. What would this do to Jorn and Cort? And to her and Becan. Would three of them eventually sicken as one took all the power?

"We need to find somewhere safe to meet Tathen and Starne," Becan said. *"We can't walk all the way to the far north. That would take too long."*

"When can we enter the sacred waters again?"

Morgane followed the direction Becan and Cort took, remaining at Jorn's side.

He didn't answer immediately. *"Not until a full day has passed."*

Morgane wanted to protest. What if something happened to them in the meantime?

They found a clearing well out of sight of the entrance to the sacred waters. Starne and Tathen landed and Becan turned into a dragon. The six of them headed north, the air growing colder the further they travelled. As the afternoon wore on, the country below them became mountainous and the snow became thicker on the ground, also coating the trees. In the distance, they spotted wyverns, large creatures flying through the skies.

"How much further are we travelling?" Cort asked. *"It's getting colder the further we go north. At this rate, the air will freeze in our lungs."*

Jorn chuckled. *"I don't think that's possible."*

"How would you know? Have you been this far north before?" Cort asked.

"No one goes this far north," Jorn said. *"Or at least if they have, they didn't survive to come back and tell anyone about their journey. Nor has anyone ever faced the creatures of nightmares, only seen them from a distance."*

"How are we going to prove we came north?" Cort

asked. *"It was different when the village was under attack. There were a lot of people who could vouch for our claims."* He made a sweeping gesture with his hand towards the north. *"Out here, it's only us and whatever creatures we might encounter."*

"We'll worry about that later." Morgane frowned as she tried to focus on finding the heart of her brother. It seemed impossible. She didn't have enough power to search the distance she needed while wearing the bracelet. It wasn't as bad as it had originally been, but she still couldn't access all her abilities to their full extent.

"How are we meant to find a heart in this country?" Tathen asked. *"It's like looking for a needle in a haystack."*

"Why would a needle be in a haystack?" Cort asked. *"Seems like an illogical place to look for one."*

"It's a saying from one of the worlds we've hunted in," Starne said. *"It's not actually about looking for a needle in a haystack, more about the impossibility of finding one in a haystack if there happened to be a needle in one."*

"Still seems like a strange place to look for a needle," Cort said.

Morgane smiled at the rumbling growl filling Starne's thoughts. Her smile faded. Was Tathen right? Was this an impossible task? She forced the fear from her, refusing to accept defeat. She wasn't about to let Brigitte have another slice of Gwynham's heart. Rummaging in her belt pouch, she took out several pieces of shaved bone, eating them. Power rushed through her, but it wasn't enough.

"Whoa, how about a warning in future?" Cort asked.

"Sorry." She hadn't considered it might be a problem for the other three. *"Are you all right? The three of you?"*

"What happened to you in that cave?" Starne asked. *"You all smell and feel different. Like energy. More so after whatever Morgane just had."*

"Things didn't exactly go the way we planned." She didn't want to explain what had happened. Not that she was exactly certain what had happened to them.

"Although they're better than we planned," Becan said. *"And if you can, have some more of that. My range has increased dramatically. Let's see if it can be increased further."*

"This is your warning, Cort." Morgane took more dragon bone from her belt pouch, glad she'd put a lot in there. She hadn't wanted to run out and risk Jorn's life. More power filled her, her skin feeling like it would explode from the power crackling underneath

it. *"I don't know if I can have much more, not without my skin coming apart."*

"I feel like I could fly," Jorn said.

"So do I," Cort said.

"Don't either of you dare try," Morgane warned. *"No one can turn into a dragon if they haven't been born one."*

"We don't know that for certain," Jorn said. *"How many hunters have bound themselves to dragons?"*

"I can catch you if you want to try," Starne offered.

"Yes." Jorn threw himself off the back of the dragon.

"No!" Morgane screamed the word throwing herself after Jorn, trying to shapeshift. Wings burst from her back, tearing through her shirt and forcing the cloak from around her shoulders so it fell to the ground below, pushing her bow out of the way. Before she could grab hold of Jorn, wings burst from his back, tearing his clothes and knocking his cloak and bow out of the way. Unlike her cloak, his remained partially in place. She saw the shock in his eyes as he continued to drop, his wings remaining out but unmoving. She flew towards him, Starne also flying in fast.

"Wings have to move to work," Becan thought to them.

Morgane wrapped her arms around Jorn's waist,

halting his plummet to the ground below. *"They need to rise and fall to keep you aloft."* Starne circled them, remaining close.

"Do you think I'll be able to do that?" Cort asked, excitement clear in his words.

"Raise and lower your wings, Jorn." Morgane struggled to keep the two of them aloft, her own wings beating hard.

"I can't figure out how they should work." Movement shivered through Jorn's wings. They neither opened nor closed, raised or lowered.

"It's like raising and lowering your arms. But more like using your shoulder blades." Speaking aloud, she tried to keep the fear from her tone, not wanting him to know how hard she found it to remain aloft. As a dragon it was simple, as mostly human, it was far different.

"What is wrong?" Jorn asked.

Chapter Twenty-Five

Morgane continued to hold tightly onto Jorn. She should have known it would be impossible to keep her fears from him. "Fly, Jorn. Please try."

"I am trying. It's different to magic." A shudder ran through his wings a moment before they moved up and down.

"Should have learned to fly from the ground," Cort said.

"I couldn't work out how to make them form." Jorn grinned as his wings moved up and down. *"Nothing like the fear of death to help you figure out how to do something in a hurry."*

Morgane glared at him. *"Are you ill again?"*

"I think you'd be best pleading insanity." There was humour in Becan's tone.

It made Morgane send a glare in his direction. *"This*

is not in the least amusing. He could have died." She didn't want to think about the pain she'd feel if that happened.

Jorn's arms wrapped around her, his wings finally moving properly and helping keep them aloft. He leaned in close, his lips a breath away from hers. "Your death would pain me too."

She was tempted to protest out of annoyance. But he'd know the words weren't true. She could feel his emotions more clearly pressed against him. Like there was no actual point where her emotions began and his ended.

"Wyverns coming in from our left," Tathen warned.

"You need to get back on Starne." Fear rushed through her at the thought of how vulnerable he was. Her senses heightened and for the tiniest of moments, she sensed her brother off to the right.

Starne glided underneath Jorn who dropped onto his back when Morgane let go of him. *"Do we fight or fly?"* Starne angled so that he could see the oncoming wyverns.

She could tell by his tone that he wanted to stay and fight. But she needed to learn if what she'd sensed was true. *"This way."* She headed for the right. *"I sensed Gwynham."* She felt those she had a connection with follow her.

"How far away?" Becan flew at her side. *"And do you want me to carry you again?"*

"I don't know the distance. I only know the direction." She landed on his back, the wings sinking into her flesh. She smiled. It reminded her of what it was like to change only her hands into claws.

"Will I be stuck with these wings forever?" Jorn asked. *"That's going to make it difficult any time I want to visit my sister."*

She started to protest his words. Once they'd figured out how to break their union he'd return to the village. To his people. There were other things to focus on for now. Like helping him appear human again. She had no idea how to explain the process of shapeshifting so she shared several instances with him of when she'd shapeshifted, focusing on the sensations and feelings. She shared it with Cort in case he ever figured out how to change. If he had that capability.

"You should have shared that with me earlier," Jorn said. *"It would have made things easier. Maybe you should teach me how to fly by using that method instead of words."*

"I think I can do that." Excitement was threaded through Cort's words.

"We don't have time for playing," Becan warned. *"Those wyverns are giving chase."*

"No practising until we're on the ground," Morgane ordered. She didn't need to see Cort plummeting towards the ground.

"We might have to fight them," Tathen said.

Morgane would have preferred he hadn't sounded so enthusiastic. *"We'll see if we can lose them first."*

"I doubt that'll be possible." Becan angled so he could see the wyverns that continued to trail behind them. *"Did you and the hunters want to fly ahead and leave Starne, Tathen and me behind to take care of the wyverns?"*

"No." She didn't even need to think about it. *"No one is going to be left behind. And certainly not to face six wyverns."*

Tathen, who was in the lead, spoke. *"We might have to fight them. There seems to be another two ahead of us, in the direction we're taking. Might be easier to face these ones before we risk running into overwhelming numbers."*

Morgane almost growled in frustration. She just wanted to find Gwynham's heart. Not have all these interruptions.

"You and Becan can fly ahead," Jorn offered.

"Why does everyone think I'd be willing to leave any of you behind?" Morgane demanded.

"We know how much you want to find Gwynham's heart," Jorn said.

"Not at the expense of the living." She did the partial shift of earlier, wings rising from her back, and launched into the air. *"We'll take out these ones. Then we take on the ones ahead."* The ones that were between her and Gwynham's heart.

"I'm sure I could shift to part dragon too," Cort said.

Morgane glanced over her shoulder, continuing to fly towards the wyverns. *"Not until you're on the ground."*

Jorn readied his bow, drawing back an arrow. *"Use the techniques you're accustomed to. Time enough to learn new ones later."*

Relieved to see Cort ready his bow, Morgane put on a burst of speed. She started to reach for her dagger, stopping and attempting to change her hands into claws. As they started to form, she struggled to maintain her wings. Forgetting about claws, she focused on wings, now concerned she might be the one that plummeted to the ground.

Becan shot ahead of her, attacking the wyverns before she could. His claws slashed at wings as he avoided the barbed tails that swung towards him.

Morgane drew her dagger, attacking a wyvern that aimed for Becan's back. She slashed at the wings, slicing them into strips. The wyvern tried to grab hold of her as it lost height, its barbed tail swinging towards her face. With one last slash at its wing, she flew out of the way.

The wyvern's screech was cut off abruptly as it collided with the ground below. Another wyvern crashed beside it, riddled with arrows.

Two wyverns came at Morgane and she slashed out at one as she automatically put up a hand to block the other one. A force of air pushed it back, causing it to tumble through the air, trying to regain the use of its wings. "That was magic? I used magic?"

"Behind you," Jorn warned.

She spun to face the other direction, raising both hands, the left one held open. Not knowing how she'd used magic the previous time, all she could do was strike out with her dagger.

Becan dropped onto a wyvern, his claws raking through the membranes of the wings. *"What happened to waiting to learn the new skills. If Cort needs to be on the ground before he can practice, then you shouldn't be in a fight when you practice either."*

Morgane threw back her head and laughed, the wyvern that had attacked her plummeting to the ground below. She held up the dagger. *"This is the weapon I'm accustomed to."* She glanced at her left hand. *"The other, it was unplanned."* She turned to face the rest of her companions, her gaze examining each of them as she made sure they were unharmed. A glance at the ground below showed it was littered with the six wyverns. *"Ready to go after the other two?"*

Cort grinned. *"This is why I came with you."* He paused a moment. *"Well, one of the reasons."*

Morgane landed on Becan's back, her wings drawing in and once more becoming part of her back. She was more fatigued than usual. Flying as a human wasn't as simple as flying as a dragon. *"Remain vigilant. Brigitte will have chosen an area that's dangerous to reach. She won't want just anybody trying to take the heart from her."*

It didn't take long to reach the wyverns Tathen had spotted. They swooped down on them, outnumbering and outmaneuvering the creatures. They saw more in the distance. Four of them.

"Do you think I'd be able to take the head of one of them?" Cort asked as they flew towards their next opponents. *"There's no way anyone is going to believe we've faced and conquered these creatures."*

Morgane's gaze narrowed and she stared at the creatures ahead. *"I want to take some of the heads back and drop them on the battlements of Brigitte's castle. Let her know we went north. Let her wonder why."*

"That would be a good tactic," Becan said. *"Keep her wondering about the meaning behind your message. We'll gather some before we return south."*

There was no time to discuss the plan further. The wyverns ahead of them spotted them and streaked towards their group. The battle was nearly over when Morgane once more could sense her brother. They were getting close. Excitement raced through her. Brigitte wasn't going to keep her from finding Gwynham's heart. No matter how dangerous the area. She'd fight through whatever was between her and her goal.

"What are you thinking of?" Jorn asked. *"You have that same emotion you had at the thought of capturing the castle."*

"I was thinking of Brigitte. And finding Gwynham's heart." Landing on Becan's back, she grinned at Jorn. He remained on Starne's back, the dragon keeping pace with Becan.

Jorn laughed. *"I should have known. We will make her pay for all she's done."*

"We'll take her castle," Becan promised.

"I'll be in on that," Cort said. *"I wouldn't mind seeing those gold plates you eat off."*

Morgane looked from Jorn on her right to Cort on her left. *"I don't think the two of you realise exactly how dangerous it would be to try and capture a castle."*

"The danger is why I'm interested," Cort said.

When Jorn didn't answer, Morgane looked towards him. *"And you? Is it the danger that makes you want to capture the castle with me?"*

He smiled at her. *"You know why, Morgane. Nothing has, or will, change."*

A shiver ran through her at his words. At his promise. She wanted to protest. She wanted to make her own promises. Wanted to hear similar promises back from him. Dragon promises that no human would know how to make. Her gaze focused on his. She breathed in sharply, seeing the promises in his eyes that she doubted she'd ever hear in his words. *"Yes."*

Jorn didn't ask her what she was agreeing to. Instead, his smile widened into a grin and he nodded. He held her gaze a moment longer before he looked ahead. *"Where is your brother's heart?"*

She focused on the area. Nothing. Having a piece of the shaved dragon bone caused power to flare through her and she was able to pinpoint exactly where Gwynham's heart was.

"What happened to a warning?" Cort demanded.

Morgane smiled wryly, half shrugging as she looked at him. *"I know where Gwynham's heart is."* Shifting so her wings formed, she took to the air, flying ahead.

Jorn joined her, his wings spread out as he soared through the sky beside her. *"I never doubted you'd be able to find it. But don't go ahead without us. Who knows what is nearby."*

It didn't take long to find out the lengths Brigitte had expected her warriors to go to in preventing others from getting the heart. Morgane leaned against the tree she'd landed beside, peering at the cave entrance where wyverns flew in and out. "We might not need to go inside, but it's almost as bad." She gestured to the undisturbed snow in front of the cave entrance. "The heart has been buried there."

"How could they have faced that and returned to the castle?" Cort asked.

Morgane shrugged.

"One would have baited them away while the other hid the heart," Becan said.

"How would the one who'd baited them have escaped?" Jorn nodded towards the wyverns who flew out of the cave. "They don't impress me as the type of creature who'd eventually give up and let their prey escape."

"They're not." Morgane watched the wyverns fly away. "Especially if they can see them and especially not a dragon, their mortal enemy."

"There must be somewhere around here that a dragon in human form can hide until the wyverns grow bored with the wait." Starne glanced around the area. "All we need to do is find it."

Chapter Twenty-Six

Morgane wrapped her arms around herself, the cold seeping into her. "I doubt it'll be that easy."

Becan looked to Starne. "You head west." He turned to Tathen. "You go east. Avoid wyverns and see what you can find. We'll meet back here when the sun drops below that peak." He pointed to the highest mountain peak that they could see.

"You can't expect them to go off on their own like that," Morgane protested.

"We'll hear them if they discover trouble instead of a hiding place," Becan said.

Tathen grinned. "I'm not about to let a wyvern outsmart me." He clapped his brother on the shoulder. "I bet I can find a suitable hiding place before you can."

Starne held out his hand, shaking Tathen's. "You're on." Spinning, he raced towards the east.

Tathen headed in the opposite direction.

Morgane looked from the east to the west, her gaze eventually falling on Becan. "They'd better return. I'll not throw away their lives, or anyone else's."

Becan held her gaze for a moment before he inclined his head. "I'll take that into account whenever I make plans on your behalf."

"Why doesn't she make all her own plans?" Cort looked between the two of them, frowning.

"Because I'm her first warrior," Becan said.

Cort continued to look confused. "I thought that only meant you put yourself between Morgane and danger. That doesn't make sense."

"It does to me." Becan turned to Morgane. "Did you want to move away from this location so I can make a fire so you can warm yourself?"

"No, I'd rather search for a hiding place too." She smiled at Jorn when he moved close and slipped an arm around her waist, sharing his cloak with her. "Thank you."

It was Cort who found a narrow tunnel that opened into a wider cave, impossible for a wyvern to enter, but large enough for a human. Starne glared at Cort when he returned, landing a moment before his brother. "The human won."

Tathen grinned. "Guess that means I won since he's my hunter."

"That doesn't count," Starne argued. "If it wasn't you or me, then neither of us won."

"Sure it counts," Tathen said. "A win by a dragon's warrior counts so then a win by their hunter must count too."

"Why would you say I'm your hunter?" Cort asked.

Tathen grinned at him. "Didn't we invade the castle together? Haven't we flown together and fought wyverns, protecting each other during that fight?"

"But why would you say that makes me yours?" Cort asked. "Why would you say you own me?"

"Own you?" Tathen frowned. "No, not own you. You're mine. Not a slave."

"It still doesn't make sense to me," Cort said.

"That's because you're not a dragon," Morgane said. "It's kind of like your hunting companion. Someone you'll protect and who you trust to watch your back and not sink a dagger in it."

"Oh." Cort eyed Tathen, eventually nodding. "I'd never stab you in the back. That's not the kind of thing you do to a friend."

Trying not to smile at how literally Cort often took

things, Morgane glanced at each of her people. "Who will draw the wyverns away? I won't make any of you do such a task if you'd rather not." She hoped someone would volunteer. She wasn't sure she could leave finding the heart to another.

"I can go," Jorn offered.

Starne and Tathen stepped forward at the same time. "I can." They echoed each other.

"What about the hoard?" Tathen asked. "Will we go after it?"

"Not today." Morgane could almost feel their disappointment, then realised she actually could feel disappointment. Her gaze fell on Becan. "Wyverns aren't the only ones who've hoarded treasure over the years."

"Brigitte," Becan said.

Morgane nodded, smiling when Becan's disappointment became anticipation. "If we take the castle, we'll also gain her hoard. All those involved will be entitled to something for their help."

Tathen shapeshifted. *"Sooner we get this done, the sooner we can take the castle and get our hands on at least one hoard."*

Starne shifted into his draconic form. *"I'm ready."*

"Lead them away. Make sure you wait until you

have all of them after you. I'll stay behind in case there are any stragglers," Becan said.

Cort moved close to Morgane. "I'll help you find the heart." He paused a moment. "It's a real heart we're going after and not something called that?"

"It's my brother's heart that was ripped from his chest and partially eaten by Brigitte and her first warrior."

"Brigitte, who is your mother," Cort said.

Morgane inclined her head.

"What's wrong with some of you dragons? I've fought with my brothers and sisters, gained and given black eyes and other bruises, but I'd never kill them. I'd kill to protect them, but not them. Never them," Cort said.

Morgane pointed at him. "There. That feeling you have right now. That's what a dragon feels when they say someone is theirs. That mess of overwhelming emotions that would have you tear the world apart to save them. That would have you rip hearts out." She couldn't help looking towards Jorn who was at her side, once again sharing the cloak with her.

He met her gaze. "Tearing out a heart seems too tame when going after someone who's taken a loved one from you. I doubt I'd be rational in a fight against someone who attacked you."

Her mouth dropped open as she realised she'd been as focused on the literal as Cort often did. "You'd…" Words wouldn't form clearly.

Jorn grinned as he wrapped his arms around her waist, pulling her against him. "I doubt there'd be enough of them left to rip out their heart."

She felt it, the fierce feeling she'd wanted from him. His methods might be different to hers, but the feeling behind them was the same. Her lips met his and she clung to him, not pulling apart until Becan warned them the wyverns had been led away. She held tight to Jorn a moment longer. "We will continue this later."

"I look forward to it." Jorn let her go to follow Becan who was striding towards the cave entrance.

Morgane hurried after him, scanning the area. She glanced at Cort who walked beside her, also looking in every direction. "You can go invisible."

Cort held out a hand. "I can hide you."

"No." She didn't want to risk anything interfering with her ability to find Gwynham's heart. She could sense it ahead of her, buried beneath the snow.

Cort lowered his hand. "I can hide someone as well as Jorn can."

Hearing the hurt in his tone, she glanced at him. "I'm sure you can, but I don't want anything to interfere with my ability to sense where Gwynham's heart is."

"So you'd let me hide you if it wasn't for that?"

She slowed her pace as she studied him. Her frown cleared and she smiled at him, resting her hand on his shoulder for a moment. "You're one of mine too, Cort. Along with Jorn, Elin, Anja, Gilda and my warriors."

"Does it bother you that there aren't many you can call your own? That you don't have many people?" Cort asked.

"By dragon standards, I have far more than most have." She smiled reassuringly at him before focusing on the task ahead. Her jaw tightened. Brigitte would pay for what she'd done. Reaching the location, she knelt in the snow, shivering as she struggled to keep her body temperature up. She scooped handfuls of snow away, her teeth beginning to chatter.

Becan joined her. "Let me." He dug in the snow.

Jorn drew her to her feet, wrapping his arms and the cloak around her. "You're freezing."

She started to pull away from him. "I need to-" Her gaze was fixed on the timber box Becan pulled out of the snow. "Gwynham." The word was soft.

Becan rose to hold the box out to her.

Before she could take it, the sound of a wyvern

screeching reached them a heartbeat before several flew out of the cave entrance. One of them swooped on Becan.

Cort threw himself at Becan, the two of them vanishing.

Morgane started to step towards them, drawn back by Jorn. The light bent around them, but she could still feel the rush of air from the wyvern as it flew upwards, coming back towards them.

"Can it tell where we are?" Cort asked.

Morgane sensed them moving towards the trees they'd hidden amongst before. The wyvern appeared to be following them. "I think it can." She ran with Jorn, veering away from where the wyvern flew.

"Why isn't it going after you? Why us?" Cort asked.

She had a theory, but she didn't want to voice it. Didn't want to admit that the wyvern might not recognise her as a dragon. Not like it recognised Becan. The rest of the wyverns that poured out of the cave entrance aimed for Becan too.

"We're not going to reach the trees in time and there are too many for us to fight," Becan said. "Why didn't these ones come out earlier?"

Morgane shrugged, letting go of Jorn's hand to draw her dagger. She'd considered the sword, but it would be too long for what she needed. Leaping into the air, her wings formed, beating rapidly as she aimed for the wyvern that was closest to Becan and Cort.

"Morgane! No." Jorn threw himself into the air too, becoming visible for a moment. His wings burst into existence and he vanished again.

The light continued to bend around her as she landed on the wyvern, slashing at his wings. He screeched, trying to spin and reach her, jaws snapping on the air in front of her. She let go, attacking another wyvern that had continued to go after Becan and Cort.

"Are we facing them?" Becan asked.

She sensed him slowing. *"Run. Get amongst the trees then head towards Starne and Tathen."* She sliced at the membranes of the wings, avoiding claws, sharp teeth and barbed tails. Beside her she sensed Jorn, unable to see him.

"You can't expect me to leave you in danger," Becan protested.

"Get out of danger and I can follow you. Protect the heart." Morgane barely avoided a barbed tail, drawing her wings in close to keep them from being slashed by the claws of another wyvern. She didn't know how long she could avoid being hit.

"Need some energy," Jorn said.

She flew higher, helping herself to some of the dragon bone before swooping back down, slashing at the wyverns' wings. Energy burst through her and she sensed the other three move faster.

"Should have done that sooner," Cort said.

"I didn't feel weak." Morgane darted between two wyverns, slashing at first one and then the other.

"Neither did I," Jorn said. *"But I soon will. Land."*

She dropped to the ground, her feet barely touching the snow before a rush of air forced the wyverns away from them, tumbling them through the air.

Jorn became visible beside her, dropping to the ground on one knee, struggling to rise.

She had more dragon bone as she directed her thoughts to her companions. *"Energy warning."* Taking Jorn's hand, she tugged him to his feet.

"Weren't you getting to safety?" Becan demanded.

Before Morgane could tell him they were about to run for the cover of the trees, Starne spoke to them.

"Wyverns have given up trying to find us. They're headed back in the direction of their nest."

Morgane tried not to let the words worry her. But they did.

Jorn's hand momentarily tightened on hers. *"Faster. Have more energy if you need it."*

"My skin can barely contain the magic as it is," Morgane protested. Behind her she heard the wyverns coming after them again.

"Then use it," Jorn said.

"I don't know how." She tried to run faster, but she was going as fast as she could. And it wasn't as fast as a wyvern. A glance at Jorn showed his wings were gone. She wasn't about to leave him behind.

Cort appeared in front of them. "Drop to the ground." He raised both hands. A rush of air was forced towards the wyverns.

Chapter Twenty-Seven

Morgane felt the edge of the forced air wash over her where she'd thrown herself against the snow. The cold seeped further into her body and she tried not to let her teeth chatter. She couldn't stop them.

Jorn staggered to his feet, taking the hand Cort held out and drawing Morgane up with him. "It won't stop them for long."

She could see the trees ahead. "It will be enough." Behind she heard the screeches and cries of the wyverns as they struggled to take to the air again. Putting on a burst of speed, Morgan reached the treeline, not slowing her pace. Ahead was Becan, no longer invisible, the timber box clutched against his chest. "Go. Take the heart to where you put the other one."

Becan opened the box as she reached him. "You don't want any-"

She closed the lid, not wanting to look upon the eighteen even slices a moment longer. Pain stabbed through her and she tried to convince herself it was the way of things amongst dragons. But she'd obviously spent too much time with humans. "No. Take it." She would eat Dorran's heart. That wouldn't bother her. She didn't know that she'd ever be able to eat Gwynham's heart. Not after seeing it sliced up like that. She shied away from thoughts of his bones. Brigitte would pay for what she'd done to them. To her and Gwynham. "We'll meet you at the clearing where we took to the skies after we visited the sacred waters."

Becan nodded, slipping the box into his dragon-leather rucksack. He ran through the trees, changing form and taking to the sky when there was a large enough gap between the trees.

Morgane turned to see what the wyverns were doing. Several attacked each other, the rest were slowly taking to the sky, headed for the trees. "We have to make sure they don't follow Becan." Morgane's wings spread and she launched into the sky, dragging her hand from Jorn's grip.

"There are more coming," Cort said.

"I know." She flew upwards, twisting and turning to avoid tree branches, taking up less space in this form

than in her draconic one. *"We only have to distract them for a short time."*

Jorn flew up into the sky beside her, a dagger in his hand. *"I can't keep us invisible, fly and use magic."*

"Then don't worry about keeping us invisible." She arrowed towards the oncoming wyverns slashing out at them. Below she could see Cort had his bow in hand and was firing at the wyverns. She dived on the ones he went after. *"We don't need to distract them for long."*

Jorn forced a gust of air at two of the wyverns who tumbled out of the sky then glanced over his shoulder. *"That's good because I don't think we've got long before we'll need to take cover."*

Spotting a wyvern trying to reach Cort through the trees, she dived towards them, not having the time to check what Jorn referred to. She could only assume it was the rest of the horde heading back to them. She slashed at the wyvern that flew upwards out of her way, no longer able to sense Becan in the area. He'd escaped. *"Time to go."* She dropped down through the trees to land on the snow.

Jorn dropped down beside her. "Probably past time. We need to head to the right before we veer to the left. If we go straight ahead, the trees thin too much for them to provide enough cover."

She ran at his side, Cort following. "I didn't think to check."

"There might be a couple of wyverns still outside the tunnel," Tathen said. *"Either that or something else has started to try and scratch its way in."*

"There's a clearing between the trees and the tunnel," Cort said.

"I know." She would have prefered he hadn't reminded her.

"How are we going to get inside the tunnel so we can wait out the wyverns?" Cort asked.

She supposed telling him she didn't know wasn't the answer he was looking for. Not with the tone of his voice. "Think of the stories you'll be able to tell of this day."

Jorn chuckled. "The suspense will keep your listeners on the edge of their seats."

Morgane grinned, glancing at Jorn.

"Are you mocking me?" Cort asked.

She glanced over her shoulder at him. "Only a little."

"Time to veer to the left," Jorn said.

They continued to race through the trees, wyverns flying overhead, several screeching their displeasure at not being able to reach their prey. Arriving at the edge of the clearing, Morgane looked up at the circling wyverns. They knew they'd be able to get them once they left cover and were waiting.

"I'll go first." Cort went invisible.

"Wait." Morgane grabbed hold of him, the light bending around her. "What if they can find you when you're hidden. Like they could find Becan."

"Only one way to find out." Cort pulled out of her grip, becoming invisible to her.

Her gaze followed his movements as he stepped out of cover, even though she couldn't see him. A couple of wyverns came lower. Her hand rested on the dagger she'd sheathed while they'd run through the trees. "What if they're waiting for him to be too far from cover before they attack?"

Jorn took hold of her hand, momentarily tightening his grip on it. "Then I will attack."

Morgane tried to count the wyverns flying above them. It was impossible. There had to be at least fifty of them. "Do you really expect to win against these odds?" She gestured to the sky above.

"No, but that won't prevent me from trying." He nodded to where both of them could sense Cort approaching the middle of the clearing. "I'd find it impossible to stand back while a companion of mine lost their life."

Before Morgane had the chance to reply, the

wyverns swooped towards Cort. "They can sense him." She grabbed the dragon bone out of her belt pouch. *"Energy warning."* She took to the sky as she ate the dragon bone. *"Both of you flee and don't hide me, Jorn."* She took a deep breath before she spoke as loudly as possible. "I'm over here."

Jorn flew up to join her. *"Did you listen to me before? I'm not about to desert you."*

"You're not deserting me." Morgane dodged the wyverns that came for her. *"I can fly faster than you. All I have to do is avoid them long enough for the two of you to get to safety and then I can join you."*

Jorn dodged the attacking horde of wyverns. There were too many creatures to do anything other than avoid their attacks. *"Do you promise?"*

She barely managed to avoid the claws aimed at her. *"Go. Both of you. I can't distract them forever."*

Jorn vanished and the wyverns focused on Morgane. *"You'd better be right."*

"This feels wrong." Even as he thought the words to them, Cort raced towards the tunnel.

Morgane didn't have time to reply. She was too busy trying not to get herself killed. Now that she was the only one visible, the wyverns seemed to be focusing their attention on her. The prey that they could see.

"*I'm at the tunnel,*" Cort said. "*Can the two of you make it? Or do you need help?*"

Still Morgane found it impossible to answer as she dodged claws, barbed tails and wide open mouths full of sharp teeth.

"*Morgane?*"

She could hear the worry in Jorn's thoughts. But she couldn't answer. Tucking her wings in, she plummeted to the ground, stretching them out at the last moment to glide past several wyverns who'd followed.

"*Answer me, Morgane,*" Jorn ordered. "*Answer me or I return for you.*"

She sensed he was nearly at the tunnel. Close enough she should be able to head in that direction without drawing the wyverns' attention to him. "*Keep going.*"

"*You'll never make it,*" Cort said. "*You're surrounded.*"

Morgane barely managed not to say something to Cort when Jorn slowed. "*Keep going, Jorn.*" She flew past a barbed tail, the air from it brushing her face. "*I'm headed towards the tunnel now.*" Relief rushed through her when Jorn continued towards the tunnel.

"*Need us out there?*" Starne asked. "*Sounds like you brought the whole horde back with you.*"

"*There isn't the space in the tunnel,*" Cort said.

Morgane dived between two wyverns, one of them barrelling into her and knocking her towards the ground. She struggled to pull up.

"I'm in the tunnel. Do you want me to make you invisible?" Jorn asked.

"Yes." She managed to pull up before she hit the ground, needing to dodge several wyverns as she did so. The light bent around her and the wyverns' attacks weren't as accurate. She flew towards the tunnel, safety so close. Four wyverns swooped down in front of the tunnel, landing. There was no way she could get past them.

"Go above the tunnel," Jorn ordered. *"Hurry. Before too many decide to guard the entrance."*

She flew upwards, hearing the rush of air force the wyverns out of the way of the tunnel. The moment it was clear, she dived for the entrance, landing in a heap in front of it. Before she could get to her feet, Jorn dragged her inside the narrow tunnel. She heard the screech of wyverns behind her.

His arms enveloped her and he held her tight. "You're safe."

The words 'for now' entered her mind, but she pushed them aside. "I hope it's not going to be a long wait until they lose interest." She held him equally as tight.

Cort was further along the tunnel, his head nearly touching the roof, a ball of light in his hands. "There's more space in the cave at the end of the tunnel."

Morgane clung to Jorn a moment longer before she let go and followed him and Cort into the cave. There wasn't a great deal of space. But it was less cramped than the tunnel had been.

Starne came forward, holding out his cloak. "You might as well get some rest while we wait for them to leave."

Inclining her head, she took the cloak. "Thank you." She found a spot out of the way, wrapping the cloak around her before she curled up on the cold ground, her teeth chattering. She smiled at Jorn, and then Cort when they joined her, lying on each side of her, Cort's ball of light resting on the floor of the cave. The warmth of their bodies slowed her shivering until she warmed enough to be able to fall asleep.

It was night when Tathen, who'd been on watch, woke them, the soft glow of Cort's light continuing to fill the cave. "The wyverns have gone. Have been for awhile. I had a look out there to make sure it wasn't a trap."

Morgane returned the cloak to Starne. "It'll be nice to return to a warmer location." Once the cold wouldn't have bothered her. She glanced at the bracelet, expecting the same feelings of anger and frustration to surface. When they didn't, she frowned. When had the bracelet stopped becoming a problem? When had it actually become something useful?

Jorn slipped an arm around her waist. "Is something wrong?"

She dragged her gaze from the bracelet to Jorn. He was the reason the bracelet needed to be removed. She couldn't put him, or the other two, at risk for her benefit. "No, it's time to return to the sacred waters."

Jorn stared down at her for a moment. "It isn't necessary. It's different this time. Unless you want the bond broken."

"It's not just you and me." Morgane looked past Jorn to Cort.

Cort glanced at Tathen before returning his gaze to Morgane. "Does that mean I won't be one of yours anymore? That I'll no longer be able to fight at your side."

"You'll always be mine." She drew away from Jorn and took Cort's hands, holding them tightly. "And you'll always be welcome to fight at my side."

Cort glanced at Jorn. "Do you want more than a single companion?"

"Having the four of us bound together might be

what has made the difference. A balance between dragons and hunters," Jorn said.

"Or it could be that the bond was created in the sacred waters like bonds should be created," Cort said.

Jorn shrugged. "They aren't always."

Morgane let go of Cort's hands. "There might come a time when you want to form a bond with another."

"The one I'm interested in already has plans to form a hunting bond," Cort said.

Morgane smiled. Anja would be pleased to know Cort was interested in her. She inclined her head. "None of us can make this decision without Becan. And hopefully, he'll be waiting at the clearing for us."

Chapter Twenty-Eight

They headed through the tunnel, Starne and Tathen going first, refusing to let Morgane take the lead in case any of the wyverns had returned. They hadn't and they took to the sky, the two warriors carrying the hunters. Morgane flew beside them, adamant that unlike the hunters, she was accustomed to flying. Along the way, they collected four wyvern heads and reached the clearing as the grey of daybreak filled the sky. Becan waited for them in the clearing.

He shared images of placing the box in the snowy ground next to Dorran's heart. Satisfaction arrowed through Morgane. It was fitting that her brother's heart should be with the heart of the one who'd killed him. Fitting that Dorran hadn't lived long after tearing the heart from her brother's chest.

"Are you going to ask him?" Cort nodded towards Becan, his gaze on Morgane.

She turned to Starne and Tathen first. "Scout the area. Remain in the sky until I call you back." Once they'd shapeshifted and flown off, she recounted the earlier conversation to Becan.

"I have no interest in breaking the bond," Becan said. "It allows me to serve you more efficiently."

"What if one or all of you sicken?" She looked at each of them, her heart lurching at the thought of one of them dying. They were hers. Each of them. Had fought by her side and protected her. And she wasn't about to do anything that would kill them.

Jorn smiled. "You can stop worrying. It's different this time."

"We can always come back here if things change," Cort said.

Becan inclined his head. "It's settled. We remain bound." He faced Morgane. "And we return to Devona and Gilda to learn what plans have begun for us to take the castle."

Excitement raced through her, as difficult to contain as the magic that had overfilled her body. She raised her chin, meeting each of their gazes before her lips curved into a smile. "All her treasures will be mine."

Jorn grinned. "You've already made a start on that.

You took her first warrior and the heart she'd hidden for the future."

"Time to finish the process." Morgane's wings snapped out and she called Starne and Tathen to her.

It was mid-morning when they reached the cave to find Devona was out and Gilda on her own. Gilda threw her arms around Morgane. "Hatchling. I was worried for you."

"Why are you alone?"

Gilda drew away from Morgane, beckoning to the edge of the clearing. Two warriors stepped into the clearing, coming forward when Gilda continued to beckon them over, their gazes frequently drawn to the wyvern heads Tathen and Starne carried. "Their mother was a dragon and their father human. Devona told them that unlike Brigitte, you actually like humans. And have friends amongst them. They've sworn loyalty to no one as Brigitte won't accept the word of those who are neither dragon nor human. She doesn't believe they can be trusted."

Morgane looked them up and down. "Can you be trusted?"

"Yes." They both answered at once.

Morgane studied them a moment longer. The similarities between them claimed them to be brother and sister. "Where are your parents?" If their mother remained with Brigitte there was always the risk their loyalty would remain with her.

It was the female warrior who spoke. "Brigitte sent her hunters after them. We managed to hide for years, but they eventually tracked us down."

The male warrior took a step forward, partially shielding his sister's body. "Our father hid us from sight before both our parents led the warriors away. That was the last we saw of them."

"What was their crime against Brigitte?"

The warriors shared a look, the female the one to answer. "Having us. She saw it as a betrayal. Dragons and hunters don't belong together. Yet she has hunters who are willing to do her bidding."

Morgane couldn't resist a glance in Jorn's direction. She returned the smile he gave her. Some dragons and hunters did belong together.

The male warrior's eyes narrowed. "He is why you go against Brigitte?" He glanced at Jorn.

"No. She took what was mine. Gwynham is why I go against her. Jorn is one of the reasons why I'll be successful."

Jorn joined them, slipping an arm around her waist. "You are the reason why you'll be successful."

She looked up at him, smiling at him again. "A warrior can fight alone. But without those at your back that you can trust, it's difficult for a warrior to beat impossible odds."

Cort joined them, standing on the other side of Morgane. "I've always liked the sound of impossible odds. No one tells stories about the easy tasks. The ones anyone can complete."

Morgane sensed Becan join them, remaining behind her, not speaking.

The warriors shared a look. Again it was the female warrior who spoke. "I'm Hella and my brother is Ari. We also have two younger brothers that we've left in a small cave not far from here."

"Cave. It's not much more than a hole in the ground," Ari said.

"Swear loyalty to us and you will have our protection. Including your younger brothers," Morgane offered.

"Our brothers aren't old enough to fight," Hella said.

"They will have our protection," Jorn said.

Morgane couldn't resist a smile. 'Our protection' sounded good to her. Especially after thinking she'd spend her life alone and hunted by Brigitte.

"Do you wish us to swear loyalty by our father or our mother's people?" Ari asked.

Morgane's smile widened, excitement racing

through her. The question caused so many possibilities to fill her mind. She could choose one race over the other or she could accept both, neither more important than the other. That was where Brigitte and her warriors had gone wrong. She'd come here wanting to conquer. It was, after all, the dragon way. But this world was filled with hunters, humans with the ability to fight back and win against dragons. "By all your people."

Jorn's arm tightened around her. "Hunters and dragons."

She couldn't help thinking of Tarben at his words. Of Elin and Anja. Tarben would never accept dragons, but this was a start. A very small start. "Yes. Hunters and dragons." She grinned. "And savages too if any of them ever try to make peace with us."

Cort chuckled. "Now that would be a story told for generations."

When Devona returned late afternoon she brought with her Elin and Anja. Morgane greeted both of them, throwing her arms around them, all three talking at once. Explanations were garbled and questions were spoken over them as they all tried to find out what had happened and share their news. Jorn and Cort joined them, the conversation becoming more confusing.

Devona interrupted. "We can attack at midnight if you give the word." Silence followed her words.

Morgane stepped away from Elin and Anja. "How is that possible?"

Anja grinned. "Tarben set a trap without telling anyone."

Elin linked her arm through Anja's, her grin matching. "He expected to prove to everyone that his brother was innocent."

Anja laughed. "Instead he learned the opposite."

Again the conversation became confusing, all of them with their own questions that needed answering. Devona interrupted, running through the plan and temporary alliance she'd made with Tarben on Morgane's behalf. He was as interested in getting rid of Brigitte as they were. Although he would have prefered a more permanent solution.

Cort gestured towards the wyvern heads that had been stacked beside the cave entrance. "What are we going to do with them?"

Tathen grinned. "Turn them into trophies to mount on the castle walls?"

Cort slowly nodded. "And one for me to take back to my village."

Morgane sent the warrior siblings to fetch their brothers while she finalised plans. The younger siblings could remain with Gilda and keep her company while they went after Brigitte. Eventually, everything was sorted and Devona left to talk to Tarben, leaving Elin and Anja with them. The rest of them ate the meal Gilda had prepared and readied themselves for the fight ahead.

Morgane took the wooden plate Gilda piled with venison and vegetables. "How much damage did your fire cause to the castle?"

"None. I only set furniture and furnishings alight. There are no areas you'll have to avoid when you attack," Gilda said.

Morgane smiled, giving Gilda a nod before she sat beside Jorn. She had no idea where Devona had procured the wooden plates from. There was a campfire out the front of the cave as well as the cooking fire at the entrance. They were gathered around the campfire, dragons, humans and half-dragons. Talking and laughing. Her people.

"You're happy," Jorn thought to her.

She nodded. A touch of sadness dimmed the happiness. *"I would have liked it if Gwynham could have experienced this."*

Jorn momentarily rested his hand on her knee. *"Would this have happened without his death?"*

She thought over his words. *"I don't know. One day*

we would have needed to leave. Both of us refused to swear loyalty to her as she refused to do the same. Who knows what might have happened.” Her gaze was drawn to each of the people around the fire, then finally Cort and Jorn. She couldn't imagine life without them. *“He would have liked this.”*

Once the meal was over, they headed towards the castle, joining up with the hunters who'd agreed to go with Tarben. The prime hunter appeared in front of Morgane who waved Becan back. She didn't need protection from Tarben. At least not tonight. Who knew what the dawn would bring.

“I owe you the life debt of my village for all you did to prevent Mikkel's treachery from destroying us.” Tarben held out his hand. “From his jealousy, at my position that he coveted.”

Morgane shook his hand. “It was for Elin and Anja. Any debt left unpaid by morning goes to them.”

Tarben released her hand, giving a single nod. “Who do you wish me to hide?”

“My first warrior.” She waved Becan forward. “You will go with Jorn, Cort, Becan, Tathen and me. We're going after Brigitte while the rest create a distraction.” Morgane smiled. “Devona has weakened the dragons with the same method we'd hoped to use previously.” This time they managed to get the dragon bone into the food, relying on Devona's ability to get into places without being noticed.

Tarben once more gave a single nod. "I wouldn't want to be anywhere else. Brigitte owes us a great debt for the lives she's taken over the years."

"You're not the only one she owes." Morgane turned to Jorn, holding out her hand. "Ready?"

He took her hand. "Yes." He bent the light around them.

They headed for the castle that was not far from them, sneaking inside as the rest of Morgane's people and the hunters Tarben had brought with him attacked. Invisible, they wandered through corridors, avoiding the numerous fights scattered throughout the castle. Yet nowhere could they find Brigitte, her close warriors, her hunters or her personal servants.

"There seems to be less than usual in the castle. Where is everyone?" Morgane thought to her people.

"We found a group of warriors trying to leave," Anja said. *"None of them know where Brigitte is and haven't seen her since the evening meal."*

"Why were they leaving?" Morgane asked.

"They said they owed Brigitte nothing. They'd sworn fealty to Dorran and have been avoiding swearing fealty to her while they decided what they should do. They said they especially didn't owe her their lives."

"Hunters have kept watch on the castle to make sure no one escaped," Elin said. *"No one would have slipped past them."*

"She would have known something was happening," Becan said. *"She's certainly not lacking in intelligence. She would have a plan in place for this kind of eventuality."*

"I went over many different plans with her," Devona said. *"None of them involved what she would do in the event she had a limited fighting force and those that she did have would mostly be incapacitated."*

Morgane stopped. *"You might not have."* She smiled. A long time ago, when they were young, Brigitte had wanted to protect them. Or at least wanted to protect them from others. *"I know where she is."*

"Where?" Several of her people asked at the same time.

Chapter Twenty-Nine

Morgane headed towards the kitchens. *"Devona, if you can capture the warriors, do so. Lock them in the outbuildings and place guards on them."* She didn't want everyone to know where she was going. One day, she might need to use this plan for herself. Had Brigitte thought the attack would come from someone else or had she thought her too young to have remembered what she'd shown her and Gwynham. *"Cort, Becan, keep track of me."*

"Where are we going?" Jorn spoke aloud.

"Brigitte's bolt hole." Morgane also spoke aloud. "She showed it to Gwynham and me when we would have been about three-years-old. Told us to only use it in case of invaders. But we often played in there. No one else knew of it and we were safe from those she sent to teach us our lessons, the hard way."

"I'm glad the two of you had each other. It sounds like you had no one else," Jorn said.

Morgane grinned at him. "I did. Your sister and cousin."

"I'm sorry I tried to prevent them from seeing you over the years." He chuckled. "I should have been encouraging them. At least when they were out roaming the forest with you, they weren't pestering me to take them hunting."

Morgane grinned up at him. "You loved it."

Jorn nodded, opening his mouth to speak. He remained silent as they entered the kitchen. "Where to now?"

Morgane looked around. The remains of the meal preparations had been left where they were. Scattered about the kitchen rather than cleared away. Which wasn't surprising considering there was no one in the kitchen. All the humans, usually busy with their work at this time of the night, were missing. "This way." She led the way into the large pantry, moving a barrel out of the way so she could open the secret door at the far end. The rock wall swung open on silent hinges, the room behind lit by oil lamps. There was a timber table with six chairs around it and two beds along the far wall.

Brigitte leapt to her feet, having been sitting at the

table with her people, drawing her sword. Her four warriors did the same while the two hunters readied bows. "Show yourselves," Brigitte demanded.

Morgane's hand momentarily rested on her sword. She was a warrior, regardless of what Brigitte said, but the sword wasn't her preferred weapon. She readied her bow, drawing back an arrow. Beside her, Jorn did the same. In front of her, Brigitte randomly slashed at the air, her warriors doing the same. "Make me visible."

Brigitte glared at her. "I should have killed you immediately. Not left it until I finished Gwynham's heart."

"Do you want us visible?" Cort asked.

Morgane had sensed Cort enter and head to the left and Becan head to the right. She assumed Tathen and Tarben were with them. Jorn remained at her side, still hidden. *"No. But I do want you and Jorn to start firing arrows at the rest of them when I give the order. Tell Tarben to do the same, Becan."*

"Attack her," Brigitte ordered. She stepped back, gesturing her people forward.

Morgane fired the arrow, flinging the bow onto her back as she called out, "Now." She leapt over the warrior in front of her, drawing her dagger to attack Brigitte.

"What are you?" Brigitte demanded.

Morgane blocked Brigitte's attack, smiling. "I'm what I've made myself."

Brigitte renewed her attacks. "No, you're what I made you. I was the one who raised you and trained you. I was the one who shackled you." Brigitte gestured towards the bracelet.

Morgane's smile didn't falter. "Gilda was the one who raised me. You ordered others to train me. Gwynham was the one who watched my back. And this bracelet." She renewed her attacks. "You might have put it on me, but I'm the one who turned it to my advantage."

"It doesn't matter," Brigitte said. "I've already replaced you. And I still have Gwynham's heart."

Morgane laughed, slipping around behind Brigitte when she attacked again. "That's where you're wrong. We dug it out of the snow in front of the wyverns' cave where your warriors buried it." Warriors attempted to attack what they couldn't see and arrows flew around the room, none of them coming close to her. Gusts of air kept her safe. "Did you really think I'd leave his heart for you?"

"It doesn't matter. You haven't won. I've replaced both of you." Brigitte vanished.

"Hide me, Jorn," Morgane thought to him. She

moved as light bent around her. She helped herself to some of the dragon bone in her belt pouch, feeling the energy rush through her.

"What happened to a warning?" Cort asked.

Before she could reply, Morgane saw a rucksack across the room vanish and threw herself at it. Her arms wrapped around Brigitte and the rucksack was knocked from Brigitte's hands. *"Take the rucksack, Jorn."*

"No!" Brigitte tried to drag herself from Morgane's grip. "I can have more. You won't stop me."

"There's an egg in here," Jorn said. *"A dragon egg. What do I do with it?"*

"Protect it," Morgane thought to Jorn. She spoke aloud, her gaze meeting Brigitte's. "I will always stop you. There aren't enough of your people left to keep you safe if you stay here."

One of Brigitte's hunters dragged her from Morgane and the two of them vanished.

Morgane tried to sense them, but she had a feeling they'd fled. She looked around the room. Two of the warriors had been subdued, one had been killed and the other was gone. *"What happened to the fourth one?"*

"A hunter took him and hid him," Cort said as he and Tathen became visible. Cort spoke aloud. "The hunter and warrior will be long gone."

Morgane stepped close to Jorn, resting a hand on his arm for a moment, becoming invisible when she moved close to him. "Make us visible." She said the words aloud, lowering her hand when he stopped hiding them. "If only there was a way to prevent hunters from remaining hidden. Or from hiding others."

Jorn grinned. "Did you think we wouldn't have worked on that over the generations?"

Becan and Tarben appeared, Tarben stepping forward. "You will hold your tongue, Jorn."

"We're bound and I have no plan to change that." Jorn stepped close enough to Morgane that his arm brushed against hers.

Tarben looked from one to the other. "We've had enough of traitors in the village."

Morgane stepped forward, eyes narrowing as she met Tarben's gaze. "Some of your people are also my people."

"Then take them from my village," Tarben said.

"You would have war between us when we could have peace?" Jorn asked.

"Peace between hunters and dragons?" Tarben demanded. "Impossible. They're too different."

"Are they?" Jorn grinned, wings springing forth. He chuckled when Tarben took a step back.

"What have you done?" Tarben's gaze was fixed on the wings.

Cort stepped to the other side of Morgane, his own wings forming. "We're bound."

"The three of you?" Tarben demanded.

Morgane smiled, giving Becan a nod when he looked to her, a question in his eyes. She waited for him to stand with them before her wings formed and she spoke. "No. The four of us."

"Impossible." Tarben spoke the word softly, slowly shaking his head. "It must be. How long has this…" His voice trailed off and he gestured towards the wings.

"In the middle of this morning it will be three full days," Jorn said.

"How?" Tarben asked.

Jorn slipped his arm around Morgane's waist, glancing at her with a smile. "Some dragons and hunters should be together. Even the sacred waters recognise it."

"You took them to the sacred waters?" Tarben demanded.

"Yes."

Morgane tensed, ready to defend Jorn should it be necessary.

Tarben studied the four of them. "You would fight

me." He looked at Morgane, Cort and Becan. "Each of you would fight me if I attacked Jorn."

"You forgot to include me," Tathen said from the side of the room.

Tarben shook his head. "No, it's different for you. These three would attack because to attack Jorn would be to attack them. You would attack because of some oath you've given." He stared at them once more. "The magic has accepted your union."

Morgane managed not to glance at the bracelet. She nodded. "Yes."

Tarben held her gaze. "Then I can do no less." He turned to Jorn. "The secrets of the village are to remain with the village. But I will see that you are not without defences against those who would hide themselves to enter your castle."

"Thank you," Jorn said. "We'll give orders to our warriors that your village is not to be harmed. That you're under our protection."

Tarben held out his hand, shaking Jorn's first before shaking the hands of the other three. "I'll tell my hunters the same."

Morgane turned to watch him leave. It took her a moment to realise that they'd won, the castle was theirs. Triumph rushed through her, too much to contain.

Jorn chuckled. "We won." His lips met hers and he held her close, eventually pulling back to hold out the rucksack he'd grabbed. "What are we to do with this?"

Morgane looked in the bag at the egg nestled in cloths to protect it. "A blood sibling." She wondered what they would look like and if they'd be a brother or a sister. It didn't matter which they were, they could never replace Gwynham. She closed the bag. "We need someone to fetch Gilda. She has another hatchling to raise."

"I'll collect her." Tathen strode from the room at Morgane's nod, taking the rucksack with him.

"Brigitte has been spotted," Devona thought to all of them.

"Where are you?" Morgane demanded.

"On the battlements."

Morgane raced through the castle, her companions with her. They reached the battlements in time to see Brigitte disappear into the distance. Five dragons flew with her, two of them carrying hunters on their backs. "Why would she travel north? That seemed like too few to travel to that part of the country."

Jorn slipped his arm around her waist. "Maybe the wyverns will take care of the problem for us."

Morgane slid her arm around his waist, watching as

light filled the sky, a new day beginning. "It doesn't matter if they don't. We'll hold the castle against her and rescue any children she might think to raise for their hearts." Around her she sensed her companions, their emotions echoing hers. They'd won. They'd taken Brigitte's greatest treasure from her and would continue to do so for as long as it was necessary.

"You're happy," Jorn said.

She thought about his words. "Yes. I am." Again she mentally touched on each of those around her. Those she was bound to. Her people. She smiled. Their emotions echoed hers. "And so are you." Her smile became a grin as she surveyed the land about her. The castle, the pond and the forest edging the clearing. All this was hers. No one would take what was hers. Not her land and not her people. She would defend them to the end, tear out the heart of any who tried to harm them.

She thought of the hearts buried in the snow. The end would be a long time coming. She might not be able to take Brigitte's life, but she had the means to outlive her. And she would. The final victory would be hers.

"What are you thinking of?" Jorn asked. "Whatever it is, you have that same feeling you had when you first thought about taking the castle."

She met his gaze. "Us." She glanced at those around her. "All of us." She tightened her hold on Jorn as the feeling was echoed back to her from those around her. Yes, the final victory would be hers.

Free Ebook

Subscribe to Avril's newsletter and receive a free ebook. This ebook is exclusive to those on her mailing list. To find out more about this offer visit:

www.avrilsabine.com/free-ebook

*

We value your privacy and will not sell, rent, exchange or loan your email address to third parties. Your information is confidential and you are under no obligation to remain on the mailing list and can unsubscribe at any time.

Acknowledgements

As always, thanks to the usual crew who always come through for me and do such an amazing job.

To The Reader

If you enjoyed this book, why not consider leaving a review to help other readers discover it too? Reader engagement is one of the few ways that lets an author know readers want more books in a particular series or genre. So leave a review and tell friends, not only about this book but also about other ones you've enjoyed, so you can continue to enjoy books by your favourite authors for years to come.

Dreams are meant to be lived,

Avril.

About The Author

Avril is an Australian author who lives with her family on acreage in South East Queensland. She writes mostly young adult and children's speculative fiction, but has been known to dabble in other genres. You can find more information about her at www.avrilsabine.com where you can also subscribe to her newsletter to be kept informed about new releases, current projects, blog posts and exclusive news.

Titles By Avril Sabine

Stories about strong characters and characters who discover their strengths.

SERIES

Assassins Of The Dead- Young Adult Fantasy/ Paranormal

Book 1: Dark Blade

Book 2: Dragon Touched

Book 3: Society Against Vampires

Book 4: King's Request

Dragon Blood- Young Adult Urban Fantasy (with elements of romance)

(5 book series)

Book 1: Pliethin

Book 2: Wyvern

Book 3: Surety

Book 4: Knight

Book 5: Mage

Dragon Mage- Young Adult Urban Fantasy (with elements of romance)

(Series two of Dragon Blood series)

Book 1: Promise

Dragon Blood Chronicles- Young Adult Urban Fantasy (with elements of romance)

(Companion stand alone series to Dragon Blood)

Book 1: Oath

Book 2: Betrayed

Guardians Of The Round Table- Young Adult Fantasy LitRPG

(Co-written with Storm and Rhys Petersen)

Book 1: Dexterity Fail

Book 2: Goblin Boots

Book 3: Singed Feathers

Book 4: Frog Mage

Book 5: Crystal Mine

Book 6: Cursed Harp

Rosie's Rangers- Young Adult Western Steampunk

(6 book series)

Book 1: Justice

Book 2: Vengeance

Book 3: Treachery

Book 4: Accused

Book 5: Wanted

Book 6: Corruption

Mark Of Kings- Children's Fantasy

(Upper middle grade/preteen)

(4 book series)

Book 1: The Arena

Book 2: The Island

Book 3: The Assassin

Book 4: The King

STAND ALONE SERIES

Demon Hunters- Young Adult Urban Fantasy/ Horror (with elements of romance)

Book 1: Blood Sacrifice

Book 2: Retribution

Book 3: Tainted

Book 4: Premonition

Book 5: Cursed

Book 6: Feud

Book 7: Extrication

Plea Of The Damned- Young Adult Urban Fantasy/Paranormal

(6 book series)

Book 1: Forgive Me Lucy

Book 2: Forgive Me Aiden

Book 3: Forgive Me Jena

Book 4: Forgive Me Kobe

Book 5: Forgive Me Marti

Book 6: Forgive Me Dawson

Realms Of The Fae- Young Adult Urban Fantasy (with elements of romance)

The Sword (short story in Like A Girl Anthology)

Heart Of Stone

Book 1: A Debt Owed

Book 2: Marked By The Hunt

Book 3: The Magic Collector

Book 4: An Unexpected Betrayal

Book 5: Imprisoned By Iron

Fairytales Retold (Short Stories)

Snow-White And Rose-Red

The Twelve Brothers

The Light Princess

Beauty And The Beast

Sleeping Beauty

Aschenputtel

The Golden Bird

The Frog Prince

The Death Of Koshchei The Deathless

Myths And Legends Retold (Short Stories)

Ion, Son Of Apollo

Sir Gawain And The Maid With The Narrow Sleeves

Princess Ilse, The Giant's Daughter

YOUNG ADULT NOVELS

Young Adult Fantasy (with elements of romance)

Elf Sight

Earth Bound

Young Adult Urban Fantasy

Stone Warrior (with elements of romance)

The Jungle Inside

Young Adult Contemporary (with elements of romance)

Through Your Eyes

The Ugly Stepsister

Perfect Little Princess

Young Adult Contemporary/Paranormal

Whispers In The Dark (with elements of romance and same sex relationships)

Over Too Soon (with elements of romance)

Young Adult Sci-Fi

Experiment X-One-Six (Urban Sci-Fi/Superheroes)

An Endless Dawn (Post Apocalyptic Sci-Fi)

CHILDREN'S BOOKS

Dragon Lord (Preteen/early teens) (Fantasy)

The Irish Wizard (Upper middle grade) (Urban Fantasy)

SHORT STORIES

Urban Fantasy

Eternally Late

Dealings With Joe

Glimpses (short story in That Moment When Anthology)

Contemporary

The Brat Next Door

Fantasy LitRPG

(Set in the same world as Guardians Of The Round Table Series)

Tales Of Inadon 1: The Disc (Co-written with Storm and Rhys Petersen) (short story in Game On! Anthology)

Post Apocalyptic Sci-Fi

Compulsive Directive

NONFICTION

A Year Of Weekly Writing Exercises (Creative Writing)

Cooking For Families With Allergies (Cooking) (Co-written with Storm Petersen)

Tell Me A Story, Grandma (Memoir)

For the most up to date details on available titles visit:

www.avrilsabine.com/books/bibliography

Dragon Blood Series

To learn more about this series visit:

www.avrilsabine.com/series/db

BOOKS AVAILABLE IN THE DRAGON BLOOD CHRONICLES

(Companion stand alone series to Dragon Blood)

Book 1: Oath

Book 2: Betrayed

BOOKS SET IN THE SAME WORLD AS THE DRAGON BLOOD CHRONICLES

Dragon Blood- Young Adult Urban Fantasy (with elements of romance)

(5 book series)

Book 1: Pliethin

Book 2: Wyvern

Book 3: Surety

Book 4: Knight

Book 5: Mage

Dragon Mage- Young Adult Urban Fantasy (with elements of romance)

(Series two of Dragon Blood series)

Book 1: Promise

Disclaimer

This is a work of fiction. Names, characters, businesses, places, events and incidents are either the products of the author's imagination or used in a fictitious manner. Any resemblance to actual persons, living or dead, or actual events is purely coincidental. The opinions expressed or beliefs held are those of the characters and should not be assumed to be the opinions or beliefs of the author.

www.ingramcontent.com/pod-product-compliance
Lightning Source LLC
Chambersburg PA
CBHW050742190726
48285CB00005B/1491